Command

Also by Mary Hooper

Historical fiction

At the Sign of the Sugared Plum

Petals in the Ashes

The Fever and the Flame
(a special omnibus edition of the two books above)

The Remarkable Life and Times of Eliza Rose

At the House of the Magician

Contemporary fiction

Megan

Megan 2

Megan 3

Holly

Amy

Chelsea and Astra: Two Sides of the Story

Zara

By Royal Command

MARY HOOPER

BLOOMSBURY

Published in Great Britain in 2008 by Bloomsbury Publishing Plc,
36 Soho Square, London, W1D 3QY

Text copyright © 2008 by Mary Hooper
The moral right of the author has been asserted

Illustrations by Carol Lawson

A CIP catalogue record of this book is available from the British Library

ISBN 978 0 7475 8885 6

All papers used by Bloomsbury Publishing are natural, recyclable products
made from wood grown in well-managed forests. The manufacturing processes
conform to the environmental regulations of the country of origin.

Typeset by Dorchester Typesetting Group Ltd
Printed in Great Britain by Clays Ltd, St Ives Plc

1 3 5 7 9 10 8 6 4 2

www.bloomsbury.com/childrens
www.maryhooper.co.uk

For the Twyford Soirée Group,
who are all within these pages

Contents

Chapter One

The first half of December was a weary time when drizzle fell continually and it never seemed to get fully light, but on the fifteenth of the month it finally stopped raining. Damp still seemed to pervade everything, however: my clothes, my hair and whatever I touched, and all along the riverside at Mortlake lay thick grey mud which had been churned up by passing horses. In the afternoon, when I looked out of the kitchen window to see if I could spy Isabelle, I noticed that a dingy, opaque fog had rolled off the river and was now enclosed by the overhanging trees. These were clammy with mist, their bare twigs dripping with moisture.

Such a dreary day was not, perhaps, the best time for anyone to come a-visiting, especially someone like Isabelle, who was extreme nervous about coming to the magician's house and had hardly set foot inside the door before. I'd invited her on this day, however, knowing that the family were all going to be out. This did not happen often, for Dr Dee, my employer, was fully occupied in his library most of the time and hardly went abroad at all unless his presence at Court was requested by the queen.

On this day, however, which was a Sunday, the whole family, including the two little girls I was nursemaid to, Beth and Merryl, had been invited to the home of a near-neighbour in Barn Elms on the occasion of his birthday. Mistress Allen, Mistress Dee's maid, had gone with them, and Mistress Midge, our cook and housekeeper, had taken herself off to see her aged sister, who lived a ferry ride away across the river in Chiswyck.

I set the kettle on the fire and leaned over the big stone sink again to see if Isabelle was coming. She and I had become friends shortly after I'd begun to live in Mortlake and had much in common – although she didn't make her living as a housemaid, but bought and sold goods at the market.

As I stared into the mist, longing for her to arrive, a shape gradually emerged, which a moment later resolved itself into Isabelle, treading carefully, holding her skirts high and wearing high wooden pattens over her shoes to raise herself above the mire.

I ran into the outside passageway to meet her, carrying a candle to light her in.

''Tis horrid out, the lanes are thick with muck,' she

said, shaking off her pattens at the door and hanging her cloak, 'and as I passed through the marketplace a cart went by at such a pace that it covered me from head to toe in muddy water!'

I looked at her and couldn't help but laugh, for not only had her gown been splashed all down the front, but her face had mud-coloured freckles all over.

'Leave your gown to dry and we'll brush it clean before you go,' I said. I handed her a clean piece of rag. 'And here's a cloth to wipe your face.'

She dampened the cloth in a bucket of icy water and dabbed it across cheeks already pink with cold, then found her reflection in a copper saucepan and, peering in it, rubbed harder. Her face being cleaned satisfactorily, she fastened back strands of her long dark hair which had come out of the coil at the nape of her neck. As she did so, she glanced anxiously over her shoulder. 'You are *quite* sure no one is home?'

'I am certain,' I assured her. 'We all went to church as usual this morning, then I made Beth and Merryl tidy and the family went off in a carriage.'

'A carriage!' she said in admiration, for carriages were still somewhat rare in our part of the world. 'I should like to have seen that. Was it very grand?'

I shook my head. 'Dr Dee called it a carriage, but I should have said it was a hired cart.'

'And they won't come back unexpectedly?'

'They will not,' I assured her. 'Indeed, Mistress Midge said that Dr Dee was so pleased to get an invitation to dine from such a noble source that he'll likely stay until midnight – or his host shows him the door.'

'Who is his host?'

'Well,' I said with some import, ''tis Sir Francis Walsingham.'

'*He!*' Isabelle's face lightened with interest. 'There is much talk of the queen's spymaster. Have you ever seen him?'

'Never,' I said. 'But I have seen Lady Walsingham, because she has been here three or more times to pay her respects to the mistress following her confinement.'

'And does she dress very fine?'

'Extreme fine,' I said, remembering the last time Lady Walsingham had called, and the shot-silk gown in brightest sapphire blue and matching cape with pink lining.

'Was she pleasant?'

'I can hardly tell,' I had to admit, 'for though I ushered her into Mistress Dee's chamber and curtseyed to her very low and respectful, she barely noticed my presence.'

'Ah,' said Isabelle, shrugging her shoulders, 'that's always the way. Who notices the likes of us?'

'Though I may meet with her again one day . . .' I said with some meaning.

'Of course!' said Isabelle. 'But you still haven't heard anything?'

I shook my head somewhat despondently. I'd carried out a certain service for Her Grace, Queen Elizabeth, and that exalted lady had sent a message through her fool, Tomas, to say that she was most grateful and that I might be called on to serve her again. When I'd first heard these words, I'd thought she'd meant that I was to attend Court and become one of her ladies-in-waiting, but that was not to be, for Tomas had told me quite frankly that only titled and educated young ladies might take up these positions and attend on the queen. Instead, however, I was to be ready to carry out certain duties for the queen as and when they might occur . . . duties which might involve working covertly for Sir Thomas Walsingham, who managed the queen's secret network of spies.

'I suppose it has only been a matter of a few weeks,' I said, though indeed I was burning with impatience and fair desperate to begin serving the queen, for I revered her highly and would have done anything for her.

Isabelle was rubbing her hands together to try to warm them, all the while looking about her. 'Such a well-equipped kitchen . . . so many skimmers and pans and cooking tools,' she said. 'And that huge table – why, our bedchamber at home could easily fit on to such a thing.'

I nodded, knowing that Isabelle's family lived in a cottage so poor that the living room barely contained more than a fire with a stew pot over. 'Dr Dee has more money to spend now,' I said – for he'd recently carried out a service for a nobleman and been richly rewarded. 'We've had meat to eat every day of these two weeks past. Even on fish days,' I added.

Isabelle's eyes widened, then her attention was taken by the shaped copper moulds on a shelf above her. She reached up to take one down and see it the better, but as she did so there was a high peal of devilish laughter and one of the moulds moved before our eyes. She gave a scream and jumped backwards. 'Magick!'

I began to laugh. 'No, it's only the monkey,' I said. 'Today's visit was too grand for him to attend, so he's been left with me.'

Isabelle had gone very pale.

'You needn't be frightened of Tom-fool,' I said – for so the monkey was called, being named after the queen's jester. 'And you needn't be afeared of being in this house, either, for there is nothing to harm you.'

'As long as the magician doesn't come back before he is due.'

'He won't!'

'Or Mr Kelly,' she said, referring to Dr Dee's partner in alchemy.

'Mr Kelly has gone to London to look for treasure in the Thames,' I said. I lowered my voice, although there was no one about but us, adding, 'He said an angel had told him where it was hid.'

'Is that really true?'

I shrugged. 'It's true that he's gone to dig around in

14

Thames mud, but whether he was instructed to go by an angel, I don't know.'

She hesitated. 'So you're sure there isn't any magick lingering about this place? No demons concealed in the chimney nor small folk in the skimming pans?'

'Not that I've ever seen!' Smiling, I took the kettle from the fire and poured hot water into two glasses which I'd previously prepared with grated cinnamon, peppercorns and bay leaves, then added a small amount of claret wine, which I'd discovered left over from supper the previous night. 'This will warm you,' I said, handing it to her.

She took some sips of it, then put it on to the table and reached up to take Tom-fool. Chattering, the little creature ran up her arms and settled himself on her shoulders, then began to pull out her hairpins one by one and throw them on to the kitchen floor, where they immediately got lost in the rushes. 'He has a very pretty face,' she said. 'Is he trained around the house?'

I shook my head, turning up my nose at the same time. 'Monkeys aren't as dainty as cats. In fact, they aren't dainty at all,' I added, giggling, as Tom-fool ran down Isabelle's arm and hung by his tail from her elbow, then proceeded to pass water.

She gave a scream and shook him off, whereupon the monkey ran up the centre of the table and disappeared inside a large earthenware bowl. Isabelle brushed down her gown with a sigh of vexation, then continued her tour of the kitchen. 'So vast . . . so much fine plate and pewter . . .'

'And there is even more of it on show in the dining room,' I said, 'for Dr Dee has had the room opened up so that he may entertain more.' I took a sip of my drink. 'Mistress Midge says he's doing it in order to attract more wealthy patrons.'

'And what type of services will he perform for them?' Isabelle asked.

'They will ask him all sorts of questions – about their health and their lovers and their money, and he will tell them what they want to hear.'

'Will he do magick?'

I shrugged. 'He'll divine the meaning of their dreams, tell what a comet in the sky predicts, cast charts to tell the most auspicious days to carry out a certain task or look into the future and tell them if they will marry a certain person – but I don't know if these things are magick.'

'And does he still converse with the dead?' she asked fearfully.

'So people say.'

'They say he speaks with angels, as well.'

I nodded. 'But only through Mr Kelly. It's he who sees and hears them. Or says he does,' I added thoughtfully.

'So *you've* never seen any spirits about the place?'

I shook my head. 'No, though I've heard Mr Kelly speak to them and ask them questions . . .'

16

'How was this?' she gasped. 'Were you invited to watch?'

'No!' I said, laughing. She already knew of my great curiosity about these matters, so I had no hesitation in adding, ''Twas by standing with my ear pressed to the door!'

'Then was he counterfeiting?'

'Perhaps.' For though, listening at the door, I'd heard Mr Kelly ask the angel many questions, I'd never heard a single reply. 'But Dr Dee believes in the truth of it, for he writes down every angelic word that Mr Kelly says he receives.'

She shivered. 'I should not like to speak to ghosts or angels . . . or to live in a house where one might be seen.'

I thought it best to move on to another subject before she took fright and ran home. 'Do you want to look at the fine things in the house?' I asked, for that was one of the reasons she was here.

She pushed back long strands of her hair, which, deprived of pins by Tom-fool, had fallen loose again. 'I'm not sure . . .'

'I will tell the ghosts not to show themselves,' I teased.

She smiled a little at this. 'You think I'm foolish, but you should hear the tales our neighbours tell about this house. Why, they say that Dr Dee is a dabbler in dead bodies and that the devil comes to supper twice a week!'

'I am quite sure he does *not* come to supper,' I said firmly. 'Mistress Midge wouldn't allow it.'

I showed her into the dining room first, for this had been freshly hung with tapestries and had a carved fireplace, new cupboard and an oak coffer. This latter I opened so that we could shake out the fine linen within, for these damask tablecloths and napkins had, so Mistress Midge told me, come all the way from Holland. The patterned turkey carpet and vast looking glass from Venice were also admired in their turn, as were the crystal glasses and shining pewter, and then we replaced everything just as we'd found it and went along the dark passageways towards the library, for I had a mind to show Isabelle the real treasures of the house.

The door of Dr Dee's library was black and hard enamelled to keep any house fires from the valuable books within, and I pushed it open and went through first to light the room's candles. I then had to tug Isabelle's gown to encourage her to come through the doorway, for she was standing there, jaw dropped, gazing about the library like a country booby at a wedding feast.

I giggled, knowing that I, too, had been just the same when I'd first gone into the room. She pointed around at the shelves and shelves of books, at the coloured glass window, at the stuffed birds and animals, at the shells and roots and strange vials with coloured liquids and did not say a word, but only gasped. And then she spotted the ally-gators dangling from chains above us and screamed.

'They're perfectly safe,' I quickly assured her. 'They're dead, and have been so since before they arrived in this country.'

'But . . . but . . . such things as I've never seen before,' she said, gazing upwards in wonder. 'And these creatures have lived?'

I assured her that they had, and at length she lowered her sight and, approaching a wall of books, stared up at them and touched some of the gold-lettering on the spines, then ran her fingers along a whole line of them as if she was playing a spinet. Moving on from these, she gazed for some time at an emerald-green bird, stuffed and poised on a branch, felt the inside of a pearly shell and stepped back in horror from the grinning skull Dr Dee always kept close by.

She pointed at the collection of glass bottles, tubes and burners which had been set up on a bench. 'What are all those things for?'

'Those are but newly arrived,' I said, 'and I think – so Beth told me – they are to enable liquids to be separated and then mixed again with certain others.' I lowered my voice again, for whether or not anyone else was present, the contents of the library had this effect. 'With the use of these, Dr Dee and Mr Kelly seek to change base metal into gold,' I whispered.

Isabelle was beyond wonder at this. 'If they can do this, then they will become immensely rich.'

'*If* they can,' I echoed, for I'd oft heard Dr Dee and Mr Kelly speak of the difficulties of performing such a feat.

I crossed the library floor to pick up the chest: the small, brass-banded chest which, I knew, held my employer's two most treasured possessions. 'Look,' I said, and my voice was hushed and respectful, for though I wasn't sure of Dr Dee's capabilities as a magician, I knew from past experience that this chest contained two precious objects with mysterious and unfathomable qualities.

'What's inside?' Isabelle asked. 'Treasure?'

'More than that: *this* box holds the show-stone and the dark mirror.'

Isabelle tiptoed over towards me and tentatively laid her fingers upon the chest.

''Tis locked,' I said.

'And if it wasn't . . . ?'

'Even if it wasn't,' I said, 'I would not turn the key and take out what's inside.' For I'd looked in the show-stone before, and what I'd seen there had led me into danger.

I was still holding the chest when there came a long, low sigh from outside the room and Isabelle snatched her fingers back and clutched my arm in fright. 'What was *that*?'

We stood listening as the sigh slowly dissolved into the sound of whispering in the yew trees in the church-yard. ''Twas probably just . . . the wind,' I said, for I knew where her thoughts were heading.

'The wind it was not!' she exclaimed. 'It was more like the sigh of a wraith or . . . or the moaning of ghosts set by Dr Dee to guard his library from the curious.'

I shook my head. 'It never was! 'Twas but a wind dispersing the fog, or a boat horn sounding on the river.' I tried to speak with assurance, although in all the times I'd heard the wind gusting across the river or the hoots of the ferry boats they'd never sounded like that.

Isabelle gave a shudder and pulled her shawl more tightly around her. 'I should be going home now, Lucy,' she said, 'for I must be at market by six in the morning to secure my pitch.'

I own I was disappointed, for I'd hoped she might stay the whole evening with me. 'Do you really have to leave so soon?'

She nodded. 'I must be a-bed early.'

'But when will I see you again?' I asked, for my family were not living nearby and I had no other friend but her.

'Very soon! Whenever you come to market.' She went to the library door and, after looking anxiously up and down the passageway and tilting her head to listen for any sounds, stepped outside.

I doused the candles in the library and we walked back towards the kitchen, with me heartily trying to persuade her to stay a little longer, and she just as heartily refusing. At the back door she spoke to me, her face serious. 'While you're alone in the house you must take two crossed rowan twigs as a guard against magick and keep them beside you until your cook comes home, for now I've been in this house I fear for you.'

'There is nothing to be frightened of!' I assured her, but she took up her cloak and left very briskly indeed, and before we'd even tried to clean her gown.

When she'd gone I made up the fire in the kitchen and sat before it thinking of my life, wondering about Ma and my family and how they were all faring, and also when I might see the queen's fool again, for he'd been merry and charming to me – and besides, had silvery-grey eyes – and I'd liked him very much. Thinking on him, I naturally thought of Her Grace, and felt for the little token that I always wore on a ribband around my neck. This was but a forged coin, worthless in itself, but bearing the queen's image and therefore very precious to me, for I had long held our queen in the highest regard and, as a child, it had been my one desire to serve her.

I closed my eyes, allowing my thoughts to drift and settle (which was a great luxury, for my life did not usually offer such a time) and not long after there was thumping and swearing in the outside passageway which told me that Mistress Midge had arrived back from seeing her sister.

She flung open the back door: large, red-faced and furious, crying, 'Would you ever believe such robbery?'

I looked at her expectantly, not a bit surprised at her

manner, for Mistress Midge was a woman prone to tempers and tantrums.

'That knavish no-good ferryman charged me three pence to bring me across the river in the fog! Three pence! And then he had the gall to hold out his scurvy hand for a tip, telling me that the weather was so bad he shouldn't have been out at all.'

'It *is* horrid . . .' I began.

'Horrid? Lord above, I've known it ten times worse than this. My father was a ferryman and he went out in gales so fierce they could lift a body off her feet! Tonight? Pah!' She spat into the fire. ''Tis nothing!'

I hid a smile as she stamped around the kitchen, swearing to herself, scratching and muttering, at length finding a piece of cake in her pocket and stuffing it in her mouth. After a few moments of this she went to the barrel and poured herself a glass of small beer, then pulled up another stool in front of the fire.

'Is your sister in good health?' I now felt it safe to enquire.

She nodded. 'As fine and sprightly as ever she was. And she sixty years old and more!'

'And has she set eyes on the queen of late?' I asked, for her sister was a washerwoman at Syon House, a noble household where the queen was sometimes a visitor.

'Not lately – but what do you think?' She paused and took another mouthful of beer. 'Her Grace has another suitor, and he's a Frenchman and Catholic to boot!'

I gasped at this, knowing there would be much dissent amongst the people if she should marry a Catholic.

'They say he's a short man with a pock-marked face, but has won the queen's heart with his elegant conversation and a bag of pearls.'

'Never! But what of the other suitors?' I asked eagerly, for the queen's romantic associations were a great conversation piece amongst us all. 'What about the Earl of Leicester?'

'Exactly. *What* about the Earl of Leicester?' Mistress Midge said. 'They say he's broken-hearted and hasn't been at Court for days. And what of Francis Drake, back from his travels and set to woo the queen? And young Oxford?'

'And Walter Ralegh?' I reminded her.

'Indeed!'

We made ourselves comfortable in front of the fire while we waited for the Dee family to return, looking forward to an evening spent talking of Her Grace, of whom she might marry and whether or not it was too late for her to provide the country with an heir. And, that night at least, I didn't think any more about the strange noise I'd heard.

Chapter Two

'You should not have done such a thing,' I heard Dr Dee say as I entered the library the following morning to make up the fires. He was dressed as normal in the long black robes of a scholar, and had a skullcap perched atop of grey hair so long that it tangled with his beard. The beard and tangled hair made him look far older than he really was, for his eyes were still as piercing a blue as the eyes of his two daughters. 'Indeed you should not have done it. 'Tis too risky for a man in my position.'

'Tush! You must take these opportunities where you can,' said Mr Kelly, who was much younger and sharper of feature, with trimmed beard in gingery-brown. 'Besides, we need money in order to achieve our goals. There is costly equipment we need. We must lay out gold in order to make gold.'

'But to put the person in question *here*! I would

rather you had not. I would rather not be associated with such a venture.'

'You'll be pleased enough to be associated when we receive the money, no doubt,' said Mr Kelly. 'For I was told by Ariel that an occasion would present itself shortly whereby we might become wealthy, and that when that time came, we should not hesitate. This opportunity was offered by the angels, Dee!'

I added coal to the fire, trying to draw as little attention to myself as possible, for I knew Ariel was one of the spirit-angels Mr Kelly purported to speak to and I wanted to hear more.

'We must not go against the wish of Ariel,' added Mr Kelly piously.

Dr Dee said, 'Hush!' and I saw, out of the corner of my eye, him nod towards me, but Mr Kelly tossed his head dismissively as if to say I was not worth consideration. He said, 'We'll leave it a day or so for the family to get concerned about her, and then send a letter.'

'I don't like it,' Dr Dee said. 'You know how servants hear things and gossip amongst themselves. News spreads from one house to another . . .' He suddenly raised his voice. 'Haven't you finished yet?' he called to me.

I was sweeping coal dust from the hearth – slowly, of course, for I was greatly interested in their conversation. 'Nearly, Sir,' I said meekly. 'Almost done.'

'Then hurry yourself a little more,' Mr Kelly snapped.

I was made cross by this – for I was not employed by Mr Kelly and felt he had no right to speak to me so – but I merely picked up my coal scuttle and brush and went to the door, bobbing both gentlemen a curtsey at its threshold. They did not acknowledge this or even nod at me, however, for they were intent on speaking of money. As the door closed I heard Mr Kelly say, 'Twenty gold angels is a considerable sum, but 'tis easily come by for men such as her father.'

This was intriguing, and I walked back through the house wondering what was going on and wishing that I could have stayed and heard more. Thinking that, I smiled to myself, for it seemed strange that the very thing I'd oft been admonished about by my mother – my curiosity – was set to be of use in my work for the queen. Not, I thought, that Dr Dee or Mr Kelly were engaged on any task which might oppose Her Grace, for I had heard Dr Dee say more than once that he revered and loved her more than anyone else in the world and even above his wife.

Back in the kitchen, Merryl and Beth were both kneeling on stools at the table with their horn books, copying letters of the alphabet, and Mistress Midge was calling out words for them to write down. Every so often she'd check what they'd done and declare either that the words were excellently well spelled, or that they had been writ too hastily and must be done again. Although Beth and Merryl knew that Mistress Midge was only pretending – for she couldn't read a word –

this didn't seem to spoil the exercise. I, too, often played this game with the girls and could now read a good many things, even though I'd been unable to manage as much as my name when I'd first come to the house. *Writing* my letters, however, I still found difficult.

Mistress Midge was preparing rabbit stew for the midday meal and three furry pelts were laid out on one of the work counters, ready to be sold to a furrier down-river. Skinning is exacting work if you want to sell the pelts after, and the girls' constant pleas for new words, a hammering at the door from a tradesman wanting money *and* her wrongly cutting and spoiling an otherwise perfect coney skin made Mistress Midge suddenly fling down her knife in a temper.

'It's Mistress Midge this and Mistress Midge that from morn to night. It never stops!' she cried. She glared round at us. 'We had a proper butcher at the old house!' she declared – for she had once worked at the house of Mistress Dee's parents. 'And a fishmonger and a pastry cook and a baker and two butlers and Lord knows who else, but here I'm supposed to do everything. Why, in a proper and noble household the housekeeper wouldn't have to lower herself to skin rabbits!'

'No, I'm sure she wouldn't,' I said, trying to placate her.

'It was one person for each job and each job for one person. The baker wouldn't be expected to sweep floors, the poulterer wouldn't gut fish and the lady's maid wouldn't despoil her dainty self by emptying the night stools into the river!' She wiped her bloody hands on her apron. 'But here I'm expected to do the lot!'

The girls and I rolled our eyes at each other, for such complaints were commonplace with Mistress Midge – although I knew the magician's household *was* unusual in employing so few servants. This, Mistress Midge had informed me more than once, was because most servants were lily-livered creatures who took fright on hearing strange noises in the night, or, upon seeing a shadow or a mouse flash along the wainscoting, would convince themselves that they'd seen an apparition. The other reason was that until quite recently the household of Dr Dee had been a very poor one for, as the role of queen's magician was dignified by no fee or salary, there was never any money to spare for servants.

I'd come to the house by chance; I'd been walking along the riverbank towards London in order to find work, and had come across Beth and Merryl in trouble on the foreshore. Dragging them out of the mud, I'd found myself in the happy position of being offered a job as their nursemaid, and had been here ever since. I missed my ma sometimes, and my sisters, but my father had been one of the main reasons I'd left home, and I didn't miss him a jot.

'I do *the lot*!' Mistrress Midge repeated bitterly. 'I gut fish, joint poultry, bake bread, clean the house, wash linen, tend that animal and brew beer! It's a wonder they don't stick a broom up my fundament and ask me to sweep the floor as I go along.'

Beth and Merryl giggled at this, knowing, of course, that she spoke the truth, for until I'd been taken on, Mistress Midge had also looked after them.

'And when do I get a little time for myself?' she demanded. 'I work twenty-four hours in every twenty-eight!'

'But there are only twenty-four hours in a day,' Merryl pointed out.

Mistress Midge glared at her. 'There may be only twenty-four hours in your day, but in mine there are twenty-eight.'

'There cannot possibly be . . .' Beth began, and I, thinking quickly to change the subject and soothe her ruffled feelings, began asking the girls about the birth-day party they'd attended the day before. I was immensely curious about the famous Walsingham family.

'They live on Barn Elms,' said Beth, 'which is a large estate.'

'With a park containing many fine and expensive trees from all around the world,' put in Merryl, who, although only five years old, was a sensible and serious child. 'The house is noble and very large, and built in the shape of an "E", which is for the first initial of the queen's name.'

'And there are a good many servants, too, no doubt!' said Mistress Midge, before huffing a great deal and then returning to her rabbits.

'There are as many servants as there are rooms,' said Beth. 'About nine hundred.'

'Silly! There are not that many servants in the world!' said Merryl.

'And how were the Walsingham children?' I asked quickly. 'Were they fun to play with?'

'No, they were not!' both girls said together.

'We had to stay all the day in the nursery wing,' Beth said, 'and weren't allowed about the house on our own.'

'There were six children and they all kept hiding from us. And they spoke French the whole time and said we were babies because we did not!'

'Then that was very horrid of them,' I said.

The handbell from upstairs rang, indicating that either Mistress Dee or Mistress Allen wanted something, and I spoke up quickly, saying I'd go with the girls and see what was required.

They ran ahead of me up the stone staircase to their mother's chamber and I followed at a more leisurely pace, pausing on the first step by the window which overlooks St Mary's Church, for it was there, in the church porch, that I'd last seen Tomas, and it was there that he'd told me I'd be given secret work to do for the queen. On parting from him – I felt my face flush with pleasure as I remembered – he'd pressed a kiss into my palm, telling me to keep it safe until next we met. It may have been foolish of me, but I'd looked for him almost every day since, for as the queen and Court were still at Richmond Palace, I knew he must be nearby. Looking for Tomas wasn't as easy as it sounds, however, for he was usually in disguise and I'd been fooled by him before, so I always took special care to be charming towards any young men concealed in strange garb, or those who wore hooded cloaks so that their faces couldn't be seen.

I smiled, thinking of the kiss, and then the smile dropped from my face, because suddenly I could hear the sound again: the eerie, sighing sound. So faint was it, however, that had I not already heard it on the previous evening, I might never have noticed it. Startled, I looked out of the window to see if the yew trees in the churchyard were moving in the wind, or if I could spy anything else which might have made such a sound. I could see nothing, though, no tree, bush or tall grass moving, no cat, dog or pig amongst the tombstones.

A tingle ran down my spine. Was it something truly evil? A demon set free by Dr Dee, unable to find his way back to the spirit world? For – as Isabelle frequently told me – when necromancers meddled with the dead, such things were a possibility.

'Lucy!' Merryl's voice called high and far away, breaking into my thoughts, and I roused myself and hurried up the stairs to Mistress Dee's bedchamber. I'd think on the likely cause of those strange sounds later.

The mistress of the house was younger than Dr Dee by some thirty years, but was not a well woman. She'd recently been confined and consequently was still weak, although the babe, Arthur, was with a wet nurse. I hardly saw her out of her rooms, for she took all her meals within them and – when she was not in her bed – spent her time quietly, darning stockings or embroidering clothes for the newborn. Her personal maid, Mistress Allen, was like a shadow of her mistress but much more sour-faced, and they hardly moved but together.

Mistress Dee was out of bed on this day, however, and sitting by the fire, wearing a faded wrap. Built very slight, she was sad of eye and her nightcap, having slipped sideways on her head, showed a scalp where the hair grew very sparse and thin. Looking at her, it seemed to me that the babe she had recently birthed had taken all the strength away from her.

By her feet, the girls had emptied a tin of pearl buttons on to a rug and were making flower pictures from them. They made an enchanting picture sitting there, for they were pretty girls with the bright blue eyes of the Dee family and long fair hair which curled in profusion. Beth was taller, being the elder by near two years, but her sister was fast catching her up.

'Good morning, Lucy,' Mistress Dee said. 'As you see, I've risen from my bed again.'

'I'm very pleased to see it, Madam,' I said, bobbing a curtsey.

'And I feel much better for my excursion to the Walsinghams' yesterday.'

'That's good news, Madam,' I said with pleasure, for

she was a kind lady and – though I hardly ever saw her – a good mistress.

'We found the Walsinghams stimulating company.'

She paused here and I waited, wondering what was coming next.

'And, after seeing their six children so bright and bonny and so clever in all they do,' she went on, 'Dr Dee and I have been speaking in earnest about the education of Merryl and Beth.'

I heard these words with some dismay; I feared that she was going to tell me that the girls were going away from home to attend school, or would be taking lessons as part of the Walsingham household and thus my services would no longer be required. The girls thought the same, obviously, for Beth jumped up and Merryl scrambled on to her mother's knee. 'Mama!' she said, her eyes filling with tears. 'Where will we have to go for this education?'

'Oh, please don't send us away!' Beth cried.

Mistress Dee hugged them both. 'Of course my heart's darlings won't go away,' she said. 'But we want to engage a tutor for you both – and soon Arthur can come back from the wet nurse and all three of you can have lessons together. Arthur won't be as able as you, but he can learn his letters and colours and will soon catch up.'

I smiled to myself, for I saw her plan. Much as the two girls *were* her heart's darlings, the new babe, Arthur, was even more so, and she'd been deeply unhappy ever since he'd gone off to his wet nurse. In this way she could ask for him to be returned to her quicker than was usual.

'We had a tutor here once before, you know,' Mistress Dee said to me, 'but my husband thought having girls educated was an unnecessary extravagance. Now we have our son, and now Dr Dee is becoming more successful in his undertakings, I've persuaded him that we must have a proper tutor for them all.'

'An excellent idea, Madam,' I said, knowing that the more the girls learned, the more I might learn along the way, for – provided their tutor was a reasonable man – I might be able to sit in on their lessons and be taught alongside them.

'And, God willing, is good there may, in time, be other children in the family to be educated.'

I dipped my head. 'Indeed, Madam,' I said. It was, of course, a woman's role in life to give birth to as many children as she was capable of.

Satisfied, Merryl slid off her mother's lap and resumed the flower picture.

'When will a tutor arrive, Madam?' I asked.

'Very soon, I hope, for Mistress Allen's sister knows an able and knowledgeable man who is looking for work as a tutor, and he has been sent for. He'll take lodgings somewhere in Mortlake or Sheen and come to give the girls lessons every day.'

'Will he be a nice tutor, Mama?' Beth said. 'One who is kind to us and doesn't smack our hands?'

'He's not there to be nice to you,' said their mother with mock severity, 'but to teach you all the accomplishments that the Walsingham children have.'

Beth and Merryl pulled faces at this and began giggling, and in a moment Mistress Allen came in from her own chamber. She wore a plain brown dress, cut very straight and severe with no decoration nor ruff, and her hair was pulled back so tightly from her face that it gave her the appearance of a china-woman. The only adornment she had – or at least ever wore – was a crucifix on a long beaded chain which looked very like a rosary. Crucifixes, of course, were deemed Popish by the church and very much frowned on, so I supposed that she hid it on Sundays when we went to church.

She shook her head at me. No doubt she thought I was not being firm enough with the girls. 'The children must not tire Mistress Dee more than necessary,' she said, so I asked the girls to pick up the buttons and replace them in their tin box, and we all left the room.

At the top of the stairs, on the wall, was a sheet of metal, hard-polished so that you could see your face in it, and Mistress Dee had told me that this was there to check her appearance before going downstairs and facing the world. I, too, couldn't help but glance in it whenever I left Milady and, doing so then, saw myself much as usual: my face fair and freckled, my eyes and hair brown – the latter a tangled mess, owing to the attentions of the monkey. At home, Ma had always kept my hair neat, trimming it with the shears we used to cut leather for the gloves we made, but since arriving at the magician's house it hadn't seen shears or scissors, nor had much time devoted to it at all.

I gave myself a small smile in the mirror (my teeth, I thought, were my best feature, for Ma had got us all into the habit of rubbing our teeth morn and night with a piece of cloth) and went downstairs. I paused on the bottom stair, by the window, but didn't hear any strange noise. It was much on my mind, however. Also on my mind was the thought of how Mistress Midge was going to react to the news that the household was about to gain another member, the children's tutor, who would, even though he wasn't staying in the house, need food, drink and attention.

'She must be taken into the park while still under the influence of the sleeping draught, and care must be taken that she is left somewhere she can be swiftly found . . .' Dr Dee stopped speaking as I entered the library that evening. 'Yes?' he asked sharply.

'Mistress Midge presents her compliments and asks if you would like some cold meats for your supper,' I said, taking care to give no indication of having overheard a word.

'Yes, yes, we would,' he said impatiently.

'Meat and some good white bread,' said Mr Kelly.

'Plenty of it,' added Dr Dee. 'With warmed malmsey wine and thick soup.'

I glanced at him in surprise, for he was as thin as a

walking stick and I'd hardly seen him eat a hearty meal since I'd been there. I curtseyed and withdrew, and as I did so heard Mr Kelly say, 'We must plan the letter.'

I went back to the kitchen. Something untoward was going on, I was sure of it. Something was being hatched; some plan for making money.

I prepared the supper tray, but the children wanted to take it in to their father, so I had no further opportunity that evening to enter the library. While they were absent I asked Mistress Midge if she'd heard any strange sounds while she was about the house, but her reply was typical.

'I hear nothing and I see nothing that I shouldn't,' she said. 'And neither should you.'

'I just wondered about a certain noise and what it could be . . .'

'We are not paid to wonder,' she said stoutly. 'Nor to hear noises that we shouldn't. Just remember that Master is master and 'tis his house to do what he likes in.'

Mr Kelly stayed very late that night, until after I was abed, and though I heard Dr Dee bid him goodnight and the house fall silent, I was not brave enough to venture out of my room and search for whatever might have caused the strange noise.

Chapter Three

The bellman called just past five o'clock and I woke to an icy cold bedchamber, for Jack Frost had visited in the night and the windows were so patterned with crystals that I couldn't see outside. On rising, my breath blew clouds of mist into the cold room, and my washing water and cloth were frozen so hard that I'm sorry to admit that I didn't even wipe over my face before I put on my flannelette under-smock and warmest gown and tied a shawl tightly around my shoulders. I then hurried along the corridor into the kitchen, for this room was warmer than my chamber, the fire having stayed in here overnight. I put some water on to heat and was set to brave the cold and go to the well in the courtyard to refill the water buckets, when, to my surprise – for the family were never usually around until eight or later – I heard Dr Dee's handbell ring in the library.

Rubbing the sleep from my eyes, I went along to see what he wanted. He was still in his loose morning gown and wearing a nightcap, his long beard unkempt and feathery, but was seated in businesslike fashion at his writing table with parchment, ink and quill.

I curtseyed and wished him good morning, remarking that he was about the house very early.

'Yes, and 'tis fearsome cold,' he said. 'Make up the fire in here, will you. And I'll have some hot water. Is there plenty of coal?'

'There is, Sir, and I'll do the fire directly,' I said, thinking that the water in the well was like to be frozen hard.

He suddenly fixed his piercing eyes on me. 'Can you read?' he asked abruptly.

I thought for a moment he was asking me in an interested way, as if he might have me instructed in the art of reading, and was so taken aback that I didn't reply.

'I said, can you read?' he repeated brusquely, and hearing his tone I knew, of course, that he was in no way concerned about any lack of education. Knew, too, that he wouldn't be interested in hearing that I was learning to read – and write – through playing with his children.

I shook my head. 'I cannot, Sir,' I answered meekly, for I thought he might test me and find me lacking. Also, I had early learned in this household that I should play the simple drab whenever possible.

'As I surmised,' was all he replied, and he stared once more at the parchment in front of him. 'Make the fire up, then,' he said, waving me off.

Braving the courtyard, I filled up the coal scuttles, but – as I'd thought – the water in the well was hard frozen, so that when I lowered the bucket it crashed on to ice. I set a kettle of water boiling ready to pour on to this and melt it, and in the meantime took a scuttle of coal into the library, swept the hearth of both fireplaces and, with tinderbox, straw and bellows, managed to relight the fires.

Dr Dee didn't speak more to me, but seemed completely occupied with the document he was working on. He was obviously thinking a great deal more than he was writing, for though he was muttering constantly to himself, only occasionally did I hear the noise of his quill scratching across the parchment, and sand being shaken over the ink to dry it.

Mistress Midge was soon about the place, and the morning proceeded in the usual way: with me taking a little hot broth and some bread for my breakfast and then carrying hot washing water to all the rooms, making up fires and getting my two little charges ready for the day. After this I sand-scoured some cooking pots left from the previous day, prepared a rosehip tonic for Mistress Dee (who had not slept well because of the cold), made hot spiced wine to the specifications demanded by Mr Kelly and prepared a heap of vegetables for the dinner-time broth. Later, I was sitting with the girls, telling a tale of Jack Frost rising early in the morning to paint the windows, and showing them how to warm a coin on the fire and put it on the frost-rimed glass to make a peep-hole, when we heard the handbell in the library. Mistress Midge went, and came back to report that I had to deliver a letter, which I should go immediately and collect from Dr Dee.

I was not pleased to have to go out in such harsh weather, but consoled myself with the thought that I might see Isabelle. Putting on my warm cloak and gloves, and tying a wool scarf of Mistress Midge's around my head for extra warmth, I went to the library to collect it.

'She's unable to read, of course?' I heard Mr Kelly say in a low voice as I entered.

'Whenever did a housemaid read?' Dr Dee muttered. He handed me a sheet of parchment, folded and sealed with the Dee family crest of a scarab beetle, and I realised that this was the letter he'd been writing earlier.

'Where am I to take it, Sir?' I asked.

'Do you know the house of William Mucklow, the sugar refiner?' he said, and I nodded, for his dwelling and refinery stood beside the river on the far side of Mortlake about a mile away, and there was a sugar loaf depicted on a metal sign outside.

'The letter is for him. It's to go into *his* hands, mind, and no other's.'

'Take it straight there, for it's important. No

gossiping or dilly-dallying,' said Mr Kelly, and I gave him a simple smile, so that he might think he'd caught me out on the very thing I'd been planning to do.

At the back door I put on some canvas overshoes, but indeed would have been better off wearing my ordinary leather-soled ones, as these flapped in an ungainly manner and were difficult to walk in, having smooth soles which caused me to slip over on the ice more than once. To spite Mr Kelly (although I own it was childish of me, and he would not know) I did not go straight there, but went by way of the market in the high street in the hope of seeing Isabelle.

Mortlake was a goodly sized village with many thriving market gardens and, in season, fine asparagus beds. It also had excellent river connections to London, so that many traders sent their goods downriver in order to supply the wealthy London market. This meant, therefore, that women from a little further out in the country came to Mortlake and Barnes to sell their goods and supply what was lacking: salad stuffs, baskets of eggs, herbs, cheeses, bunches of flowers from their gardens, whatever vegetables were in season and an abundance of apples, pears, plums and cherries in their due times. There was a good baker's and a butcher's shop in the high street, and also market stalls selling pots and pans, hand-carved wooden trenchers, lengths of material and pieces of lace. Most days there were peddlers, too, with ribbands and bows, and optimistic quack doctors selling bottles of linctus and various salves mixed on the spot. The smaller traders, like Isabelle, sold from baskets and usually had different things every day, according to how the weather was or to what they'd managed to buy cheaply. It was a very noisy place that morning, for everyone was crying up their goods in order to attract more sales and a pack of barking dogs were racing round and round two milch cows, who'd set up a constant, frightened mooing.

Isabelle was at her usual place but instead of trading her normal goods – penny mackerel, garlic, cabbage or candles – she'd set up a brazier of coals and was roasting chestnuts on the fire. These were selling well, for many a housewife was stopping to buy a twist of paper containing half a dozen hot chestnuts, and Isabelle could scarce get them on the fire quickly enough.

'Here,' she said, throwing two chestnuts towards me. 'Slip these inside your gloves to warm your hands.'

I did so, and though they burned at first, this soon faded to a pleasant warmth.

'Are you here to buy foodstuffs?' she asked.

I shook my head. 'I have an errand to run. Dr Dee has asked me to deliver a letter to William Mucklow the sugar refiner.' I then added in a lower tone, 'And I believe it must be something dishonest, for I have twice been asked if I can read.'

'And you didn't tell them?'

'Of course not!'

This caused Isabelle to laugh. 'Many an employer has been caught out by underestimating his servant,' she said. 'Is the letter sealed with wax?'

I nodded.

'Then a small cinder from my fire dropped on to the wax would melt it . . .'

I gasped. 'I dare not!'

She grinned. 'If you believe them to be doing something dishonest, why not?'

'But what if they found out?'

'How would they do that?' She shrugged. She shovelled another pan of chestnuts on to the brazier, setting up a spitting and a crackling. 'Have you heard the ghost again?'

''Tis not a ghost,' I said. I knew that if I allowed myself to believe that, then I'd never have another peaceful night in the house. 'For certain 'tis not, for I've heard that same noise in the daytime.'

''Tis, then, a special ghost with remarkable powers,' Isabelle said, teasing me. 'But stay – have you heard the latest rumours about the queen?'

I nodded eagerly. 'She is set to marry a Frenchman and a Catholic and her English suitors are heartbroken!'

'You know! But did you know that he won her heart with a sack of pearls?'

'I heard 'twas a bag,' I said, laughing. 'But I must get on. I'll see you here later in the week.'

I bade her goodbye and walked through the market and down along Mortlake High Street. The chestnuts cooling and no longer warming my hands, I peeled and ate them.

William Mucklow was a Puritan and though I don't know much about such people – only that they forbade such things as gaming, singing, and dancing round a maypole – the house which adjoined his refinery was tall, plain and forbidding and seemed as if it might belong to such as he. As I approached the front door, wondering if I should deliver my letter there or take it round to the back, two important-looking men came out: physicians, I thought, or legal men. I waited until they went off then climbed the steps up to the door and knocked. There was no reply so I knocked again, several times, and eventually went around to the back of the house.

There were two doors here and one of them stood wide open, which was surprising in such cruel weather. When I tapped on it a maid ran out and hurried off without looking at me, muttering to herself. Bemused, I went in, whereupon another maid appeared, looking distracted. Her dark hair was untidy and her nose red, as if she had a cold or had been crying.

'I have a letter for your master. For Mr Mucklow,' I said.

'Give it to me here, then,' she said. 'Though I don't know when he'll bother to read it.'

'I have to give it into his hands,' I said. 'I've been told so by my master.'

She sighed. 'Who's your master?'

'Dr John Dee,' I replied.

Her eyes widened. 'Then I suppose I shall have to let

you see Mr Mucklow,' she said, 'though I doubt if letters from such as your master are welcomed here.'

'I think it's of some importance.'

She tossed her head. 'Then follow me.'

I hurried to catch up with her as she walked through the kitchen and up a flight of stairs. 'Is anything wrong here?' I asked. 'Is it a bad time?'

'Aye. It's very bad and no mistake.'

'Has there been a bereavement in the family?'

'No bereavement,' she said, turning to me, 'but the master's daughter has run away – and her maid just dismissed from her post for not watching her well enough.'

I looked at her in surprise. 'Why did she run away?'

'She has eloped, they think.' She showed me into an icy room, where our breath showed in clouds. 'Miss Charity is a very naughty girl, for it has broken her mother's heart.'

'The family have taken it very badly?'

'I should say. My mistress is prostrate with weeping. She hasn't eaten for two days nor slept for two nights, and there are fears for her sanity.'

Saying this, she left me, and I stood and stared at the gloomy tapestries on the walls, trying to make out the scenes – which seemed to be from the Bible – and thinking on what could be contained in the letter.

A few moments later a tall man with long straggly hair, mixed grey and auburn, came into the room and held out his hand for the letter. He wore a black suit in some coarse material and a shirt with a plain white collar which marked him out as a Puritan, but I thought it best to ascertain I was giving the parchment into the right hands.

'Mr Mucklow?'

He nodded. 'And you, I understand, are from the house of the magician.' Without waiting for me to speak he went on, 'I'd be obliged if you'd tell your master that normally I'd hold no truck with any person of that description, but my household is in a sorry state and my wife has pleaded that I should leave no stone unturned.' He sighed. 'You know, of course, that our child is missing?'

'I heard that news, Sir,' I said, giving him the letter.

He tore off the seal, then crossed to the window in order to gain more light to read by. I went to the door but, as I made my curtsey to leave, he suddenly said, 'No. Wait. There may be a reply.' He scanned the letter. 'Damn hocus pocus. Scrying-stone! The impudence of the man,' he said, and dropped it on to the polished table beside him. Then he immediately picked it up and looked at it again, his mouth working as if he was in some inner turmoil.

'Will there be a reply, Sir?' I asked.

He clenched his hands into fists. 'Any that I might make now would be unsuitable for a maid to hear. And yet . . .' He cursed and strode to the door, where I heard him running up the stairs.

What did the letter contain? Beside myself with

curiosity, I took a few timid steps across the room to stand beside the table. Then, my head tilted as if I was looking out of the window and admiring the frost-rimed trees, tried to pick out some of the words. It was in Dr Dee's flowing script, which was not nearly as easy to read as the plain, rounded characters of the girls, but I could see very clearly the number 20.

Twenty. The number of gold coins I'd heard mentioned by Mr Kelly.

Before I could think more on this, I heard Mr Mucklow coming down the stairs and quickly moved away from the table.

'Will there be a reply, Sir?' I asked, somewhat timidly.

He shook his head and took up the letter again. 'I must speak to my wife, but the apothecary has given her a sleeping draught and her maid said she mustn't be disturbed. Tell your master that I'll communicate with him tomorrow morning.'

The maid was called to show me to the door and this she did, on the way asking in a low voice if it was true that Dr Dee spoke with spirits and could raise the dead. My answer to this – as always – was that if he did raise the dead, then they'd be most welcome to under-take a few jobs around the house.

I walked home briskly, thinking of what I'd over-heard of Dr Dee and Mr Kelly's conversation the previous day and of what I'd now discovered, and it didn't need someone with the mind of a scholar to come upon the truth: that Mr Kelly had kidnapped

Charity Mucklow with the intention of asking her father to pay for 'finding' her in the show-stone.

It had been no ghost that I'd heard sighing about the place, but Miss Charity.

Chapter Four

I had instructions to go straight into the library when I arrived back from Mr Mucklow's house and this I did, not even stopping to take off my outer clothes.

'Have you brought a reply to the letter?' Dr Dee asked as soon as I entered the room.

I shook my head.

'No reply!' Mr Kelly swore an oath and rounded on Dr Dee. 'You should have been more exact in your assertions, Sirrah! You should have told him that if he didn't agree to pay for the ceremony then she would *never* be found.'

'Enough.' Dr Dee lifted his hand for silence, nodding in my direction. 'Was there no message at all?' he asked me.

I said that yes, there was. 'Mr Mucklow said to tell you that he'll communicate with you tomorrow morning.'

'Is that all?' asked Dr Dee, frowning.

'Did you see Mistress Mucklow?' Mr Kelly asked.

I shook my head. 'I did not, Sir,' I said, 'and I found the household very out of sorts, for it appears that the Mucklow's youngest daughter has eloped.'

'That is what they think, is it?' Mr Kelly said, smiling behind his hand, and Dr Dee gave him another warning glance.

I was dismissed. Going into the kitchen I found that I'd missed dinner, so had to make do with a fish soup and some leftover bread.

I would have begun searching for Miss Charity straightaway, or at least started thinking about where she might be hidden, but the house was thrown into disarray early that afternoon by a knock at the front door and, sent by Mistress Midge to open it, I found a grandly dressed lady there. She'd just dismounted from a fine chestnut horse, and this was standing by, with a small boy holding its reins.

'Is your master in?' she asked me.

'He is, Madam,' I said, and I gave a low and regal curtsey, as befitted her apparent status, wondering which of Dr Dee's rich and titled patrons she was.

'I wish to speak to him.'

'Of course, Madam.'

I began to walk her towards the library, then changed my mind, for if Dr Dee and Mr Kelly were engaged on something magickal then they might not answer my knock. I back-tracked a little, apologising, and then led her towards the dining room, the finest-decorated room in the house. I ascertained her name, then went to the library to inform Dr Dee that Lady Emmeline Collins awaited him.

Dr Dee looked agitated at hearing this news, for both gentlemen seemed to be busy with the apparatus on the table: something was boiling in a jar, while a pale liquid coursed down a long, narrow tube and a funnel spouted steam.

'Who is she?' Mr Kelly asked.

'One of the queen's maids of honour,' said Dr Dee in some alarm.

'Shall I bring her here, Sir?' I asked, knowing the dining room was fearsome cold.

'No!' He gestured towards the things on the table. 'We are in the middle of an experiment and 'tis not fitting.' So saying, he pushed past me and, lifting up his robes, practically ran down to the dining room, with Mr Kelly close behind him.

I followed on, hearing Dr Dee say in an ingratiating voice. 'Madam! Your servant. How extreme kind of you to call,' and as I neared the dining-room door, Mr Kelly was bowing very low over her hand.

'How can I best serve you?' asked Dr Dee.

'Her Grace follows straight,' replied Lady Emmeline, and my heart leapt. 'There is something troubling her which she wishes to consult you about.'

'Her Grace is attending *now*?' Dr Dee asked.

'Immediately,' said Lady Emmeline. 'She wishes her visit to be a private one and has no equerries or gentlemen-of-arms with her.'

'Of course . . . we are honoured . . .'

By taking very small and slow steps I'd only just reached the kitchen door when Dr Dee called me back.

'Girl! Bring paper and tinder. Light the fire! Hot coals, if you please.'

'At once, Sir,' I called over my shoulder, and I ran to the kitchen to find Mistress Midge. 'The queen is coming!' I said to her with some excitement.

'Oh Lord,' she replied wearily. 'More work.'

'Lady Emmeline Collins has come to announce her,' I went on, 'and I'm to make up the fire for them in the dining room.'

Beth sighed. 'We don't have to change our gowns and be presented, do we?' she asked, and Merryl pulled a face of such dismay it made me laugh. 'I can't change my gown,' she wailed. 'You have used so many pins on me today that it would take two hours for me to get out.'

'I don't think you'll be called upon to appear,' I said, hurrying through to the back door to find twigs to start the fire. 'Lady Emmeline said it's a private visit.'

'Thank the Lord for that. Most likely they'll only be here for a moment or two, then,' Mistress Midge said. 'She's come to consult Dr Dee on the best day for receiving one or other of her suitors, no doubt. Or maybe she's had a proposal of marriage and wants to know the most auspicious day for a wedding!'

'Surely not!' I gasped.

'Though if she takes my advice she'll stay single, or else find herself ruled by a man. What use is marriage to a woman as powerful as she?'

'She says she's married to England,' Beth said. 'Though I don't know how anyone could be married to a country.'

I found the stuffs I needed and when I hurried back into the dining room, Dr Dee and Lady Emmeline had already gone to the front door to await the arrival of the queen.

'Quickly, girl, quickly!' Mr Kelly said. 'Or she'll be here and gone before you've hardly singed the wood.'

I bent over the fire, struggling with the tinderbox. I very much wished to see Her Grace, but was embarrassed about what she might say to me, for I hadn't set eyes on her since I'd snatched a flask of poison from her hand. It had been after that that she'd said she'd make provision for me to attend the Court and serve her further.

I was still crouched over the grate, swearing under my breath at the damp and stubborn wood, when I heard the swish of silken skirts behind me and Mr Kelly say in a voice quivering with emotion, 'Your Grace!'

I stayed on my knees, crouching low. All I could see were the soft leather riding boots of the queen: a bright daffydill yellow, with pointed toes and jewelled buckles.

'This is my esteemed and trusted scryer, Mr Kelly,' said Dr Dee.

'We trust your experiments are going well, gentlemen?' said the queen.

'Your Majesty . . . we are in the middle of an important one at the moment,' said my employer.

'For that certain stone?' the queen asked, and both gentlemen murmured yes, Dr Dee adding devoutly that he hoped the Good Lord would help them in their endeavours.

I continued struggling to cause a spark that might ignite the fire. 'I'll come straight to the point,' I heard the queen say. 'Emmeline, will you give the doctor the object?'

'Gladly!' said Lady Emmeline, a shudder of distaste in her voice, and she let loose a roll of cloth she had under her arm and allowed a small object to fall to the floor. It was within my line of vision, so I saw a crude doll, about six inches tall, dressed in a rich scrap of fabric and undoubtedly supposed to represent the queen, for it had red wool hair over its inked-on features and, most telling of all, a simple paper crown, painted gold, on its head. Disturbingly, however, this poppet queen was a horrid sight, for it had pigs' bristles stuck into its eyes.

Gazing at it, Mr Kelly tutted in dismay and Dr Dee gave a growl of distaste.

By now, I'd caused a spark from the box to light a scrap of paper and when I was certain it wouldn't go out, I rose to my feet and, my eyes still lowered, began to back out of the room to fetch some hot coals.

'One of our maids found this outside the window of our chamber,' the queen was saying as I left the room. ''Twas placed by a follower of the Scots queen, we wager.'

'Perhaps so, Madam,' said Dr Dee, still staring at the object on the floor.

I was at the doorway by this time but had to leave the door open, of course, so that I could come back quickly with the hot coals.

'We made light of the tawdry thing, but would ask you if such an object has any power,' I heard the queen ask.

'None whatsoever, Your Grace,' Dr Dee replied. 'It is merely a toy made by some vulgar and ignorant quack. The only power it has is the capacity to cause disquiet in the mind of whoever receives it.'

'Then we are hearty glad to hear it,' the queen replied stoutly, 'and it will not now cause us any unease.'

I heard this, then ran down the corridor towards the library, where I took up a shovel full of hot coals from the grate and carefully carried these into the dining room. As I entered, the queen was turned away from me and speaking to Mr Kelly, therefore enabling me to gaze at her and take in every aspect of her appearance. I saw that her outermost garment was a short black velvet cape, lined in fur, this being thrown back over one shoulder to reveal a wool riding suit in bright turquoise. On her head she wore a canary-yellow felt hat which bore several jaunty ostrich feathers, and all most wonderful and elegant.

'Will you be seated, Your Grace?' Dr Dee asked, gesturing towards one of the new, carved settles.

'We will not stay longer, thank you kindly,' said the queen. She took a step to the door. 'Oh, but, good Dr Dee, one more thing – we know that you are oft consulted on the meaning of dreams . . .'

I saw Dr Dee bow in acknowledgement of this.

'And though we are of the opinion that dreams are, in fact, like thoughts and are entirely of a random nature, there is one which we have had several times lately and which we would like you to interpret.'

'At your service, Your Grace . . .'

'It involves fish.'

Still bent over the fire rearranging coals, I wanted to giggle, but of course did not.

'To dream of a shoal of fish is a sure sign of wealth to come,' said Dr Dee with great assurance.

'Especially if they are silver or gold,' put in Mr Kelly quickly.

The queen laughed. 'Then that's good! The next time we dream of them we will try to ascertain the colour.' I was aware of her skirts swishing around on the polished wood floor, then knew that she was looking at me.

'Girl, what say you to dreams?' she suddenly asked, a merry inflection to her voice.

I struggled to get off my knees quickly, then immediately bent down into a low curtsey. 'What . . . what say I?' I stuttered, for it had been a dream which had led me to the queen before – a dream that she was about to take poison. 'I believe dreams *can* foretell the future, Your Grace,' I said, 'but if I dreamed of fish 'twould merely mean that the day is Friday and I am going to eat boiled mackerel.' Both she and Lady Emmeline smiled at this. I rose from the curtsey but remained with my head lowered, wondering if Her Grace remembered me from my previous visit to the palace. Was that why she'd addressed me? Or would the sheer number of people she met each and every day, the vast number of faces she saw, mean that she merely thought she was speaking to Dr Dee's nursemaid, a simple girl she'd never met in her life before.

'I often dream that I'm swimming in the Thames,' said Lady Emmeline. 'Though I would never dream of doing such a thing in my life.' She realised what she'd said and gave a trill of laughter.

'To dream of being immersed in water is an auspicious dream,' said Dr Dee ponderously, 'as long as the water is calm and still. If it is turbulent, then the dream is not so favourable.'

'I can scarce remember how the water was,' said Lady Emmeline, 'but what say you?' she asked, gesturing for me to speak.

'The only time I have had a dream of swimming,' I said, 'I woke and found that my sister's little child had wet the bed where I was lying.'

As I spoke I realised – just a little too late – that it was not the thing to be speaking to a queen about, but she and her lady laughed and the gentlemen had no alternative but to give tight smiles. Bolder now, I added, 'But I've always been a great dreamer, so much so that my mother used to make me a cordial of dried cowslip flowers to take away my night-frights.'

The queen smiled at me, her face pale with ceruse, her lips rouged red. She smoothed her gloves, which were of the finest kid leather, and I saw that she had very beautiful hands, long, slim and elegant. 'You speak quaintly, little girl, and would be welcome at Court to amuse us sometime.'

I felt myself blush with pleasure, but did not dare to look at the faces of Dr Dee and Mr Kelly.

Her Grace turned. 'You and Mr Kelly will come to Court over the Twelve Days to join an evening of entertainment, will you not?' she asked Dr Dee.

'Indeed, Madam,' he replied unctuously, bending so far into a bow that his hair brushed the floor.

'Then perhaps you will bring this little missy with you.'

Dr Dee looked from me to the queen with some shock, while Mr Kelly's expression was one of pure incredulity. 'Of course,' Dr Dee replied – for what else could he say to the Queen of England?

I curtseyed again. Tomas had said that Her Grace would make provision for me to attend Court occasionally and carry out certain tasks, and it seemed that I would start the first of these soon. This, happily, meant that I'd soon see Tomas again . . .

Chapter Five

I went to my bedchamber early, just as soon as Beth and Merryl were asleep, but of course I could not close my eyes. I knew I must stay awake in order to go in search of Miss Charity, and besides, was so excited at the thought of being invited to Court by the queen that sleep was the last thing on my mind, and my thoughts were dancing all over the place.

I mused on the girl I had to find, and pondered on the reasons she'd been taken: because of the fee to be earned by restoring her to her family, of course, but also, perhaps, for the increase in prestige Dr Dee would gain by discovering, by supposed occult means, someone who was missing.

I'd known of my employer's name and standing before I'd come to work at his house, but had since realised that his appointment as court magician had been based upon past achievements, when he was young and the queen new on the throne. He was old now, and over the years he'd increased his vast knowledge (or so I deduced from the books in strange languages he pored over and the vast charts of oceans he calculated). However, he had not succeeded in discovering that which would set him on the pinnacle of his profession: the philosopher's stone which would change base metals into gold, and provide the secret of eternal youth. Beth had told me that Mr Kelly spoke to angels who'd pledged they'd reveal these secrets, but she'd also told me that so far all the revelations had been given in a strange language, using a code which Dr Dee and Mr Kelly had not managed to decipher.

Eventually, Mr Kelly went home, Dr Dee retired for the night and the house, apart from the various creakings and groanings of its timbers, became hushed. Still I waited, making myself go through the letters of the alphabet and shaping each in my mind until, at last, I deemed it safe to rise.

During the day I'd hidden away two sturdy candle-ends, and I stuck both of these on to a tin plate and found that they threw quite a reasonable light. It was blessed cold, though, so I dressed warmly, putting my day clothes over my shift, wearing gloves and a pair of thick woollen stockings, and having two shawls about my head. I then stood in my bedchamber with my ear pressed to the door, listening to the sounds of the house to make quite sure that no one was about, for I knew that Dr Dee would occasionally, on an auspicious date, rise in the middle of the night to commune with spirits. I wondered at this stage of the whereabouts of the children's monkey, and hoped that – as was usual at this hour – he was fast asleep somewhere close to the kitchen fire and would not set up a chattering when he heard me stepping out.

I only had my own senses, I realised, for believing that Miss Charity was being held somewhere in the house against her will, for it could be that the letter I'd conveyed to her father was perfectly genuine in its offer to scry for her; it could be that the sighs and moans I'd heard had been nothing but the wind. But my inner voice spoke to the contrary, and since I'd been living in this house I'd learned to listen to what it told me, however unlikely the message seemed.

Gently, I lifted the latch and pulled open the door, then began to make my way along the passageway to the library. It was in here, I was sure, that I'd find Miss Charity, for one afternoon when I'd been playing hide-and-seek with my little charges I'd discovered a small, secret chamber behind the library fireplace – a chamber that no one else in the family seemed to know was there. Later, Mistress Midge had told me that when our queen first came to the throne, those Catholics who wanted to continue to celebrate Mass in their homes oft provided a place for a priest to take cover if the Protestant church authorities called, and this was one such hidey-hole.

I listened outside the library for a moment, then,

deeming it safe to do so, pushed open the door and went in. I looked about me nervously, for the moon was shining through a pane of blue in the stained-glass window and this cast an eerie glow about the place. I glanced at the small table on which stood a skull and shuddered, for this blue light shone directly on to the domed forehead and seemed to light the hollow eyes from within.

Quickly turning my back on it, I went towards the fireplace, wondering what condition Miss Charity would be in when I found her, for she'd been missing perhaps three days now and must have been concealed all that time. She'd be very frightened, of course, and cold and hungry . . . I suddenly recalled the evening before, when both gentlemen had demanded meat, soup, good white bread – *and plenty of it*. Of course, the extra must have been for the girl! But then, if she was well enough to sit up and eat, why hadn't she called for help or tried to escape?

'Hello,' I whispered into the darkness behind the fireplace. 'Don't be frightened. I've come to help you.'

No reply came. The low, cramped space I was in gave way to a small chamber where I could stand upright and I held my tin plate aloft, bracing myself to see someone cruelly tied up, perhaps, or blindfolded and gagged. My candles revealed nothing but a three-legged stool and a few mean utensils, however, all seeming to be untouched since I'd first found myself here some weeks before.

I stood there, perplexed, for from the moment I'd known of the disappearance of Miss Charity I'd presumed she'd be hidden here. The house was ancient, however, and had many unused rooms, nooks and crannies, and she might be anywhere.

If, indeed, she *was* hidden here at all.

As I pondered this, I seemed to hear a voice calling for help, and I started up, for it had sounded so real that I feared the household would be woken. But perhaps I had only heard it in my head.

Heard it – or imagined it?

'*Oh, help me, please!*' came the voice again.

I will help you, I silently pledged, *but I don't know where to find you. Where are you?*

But there came no answer to this. I touched the walls of the small enclosure I was in: one was solid marble, the others of brick and heavy timber. Miss Charity was not hidden in this space, at any rate.

I went back into the library and made a tour of its walls, looking behind a linen hanging and gently tapping pieces of panelling. I found nothing strange: no panels slid to one side, no tapestries swung back to reveal secret doorways.

Where *was* she? I sighed. I was weary now and longed for my bed, and knew from having played about the house with Beth and Merryl that a person might hide themselves away in any one of a dozen or more places.

I began to walk back to my own chamber, taking

care that my feet made as little noise as possible on the rushes. I could not go upstairs and search all the bedchambers, so would surely have to leave Miss Charity to her fate – at least for this night. Her father would contact Dr Dee by the morning, as he'd said, and Dr Dee would then pretend to contact her by magickal means and restore her to her family.

But what, I suddenly thought, if William Mucklow, being the Puritan that he was, decided that he could not allow such occult practices as Dr Dee suggested? Would the doctor then release her, or would she stay hidden away and eventually perish?

'*Oh, do help me, please!*'

There was the voice ringing out in my head once again, and wearily I retraced my footsteps back to the library and, reaching the stone staircase, looked out of the window at the churchyard of St Mary's, its graves shining white in the moonlight. Both times that I'd heard sighing, it had been close to this spot.

I held my candles aloft and looked around, up and down the passageway, and noticed, at my feet, the glint of moonlight on metal. Kicking away some of the rushes, I saw a large brass ring recessed into the floor and, bending down to remove an amount of straw, I discovered the outline of a trapdoor etched beneath.

My heart thudded. There was a cellar in the kitchen where beer and some costly wines were kept, but I hadn't known there was another.

I stared at the trapdoor, knowing I should lift it and

see what might be found but suddenly terrified at the thought of doing so, for all at once it came upon me that Miss Charity might have expired of cold and fright and that I'd descend into the cellar only to discover her corpse. I battled with my fear for some moments, trying to convince myself that the voice in my head was merely my imagination. I was almost at the point of returning to my bedchamber.

I did not go back, however, for I realised that as well as the wish to help the girl, I had a mischievous desire to thwart the plans of Mr Kelly, whom I'd come to dislike very much. Acknowledging this, I placed the plate containing the candles on the staircase, pushed my fingers under the ring and pulled up the trapdoor – which came up so smoothly and quietly I knew it must have been used quite recently.

'Hello,' I whispered, my voice shaking. 'Hello. I've come to help you.'

There was no reply, just my voice echoing into the darkness.

I took up the candles again and, holding them over the opening, saw that there was a wooden ladder going down into the dark. Although I still feared what I might find, I tucked up my skirts as best I could and, holding on tightly with my one free hand, descended. After a moment's thought, I went back and closed the trapdoor behind me.

Stepping off the last rung at the bottom of the ladder, one thing struck me straightaway: this wasn't a cellar I stood in, but a long, narrow passageway which seemed to extend away in the direction of St Mary's Church. Perhaps, I thought, it had once been a secret route whereby a priest of the old religion called into the house to conduct a Mass could, if needs be, have gone down the secret trapdoor and along the passageway to escape. The walls were of plain black earth, shored up with planks, and the ground was rough-trodden underfoot, and here and there water had seeped in and settled into stale-smelling puddles. I lifted my candles higher, straining to see further on, then gasped aloud, for a little way off I could see something huddled on the ground; an indefinite, dark shape.

My foot slipped on a stone, making a noise, and the shape started violently.

'It's all right,' I whispered into the darkness. 'I've come to help you.'

Reaching the shape, I saw that it was a girl lying on a rough straw mattress. Her knees were drawn up to her chest and her head was bent on to them.

I touched her, making her shudder.

'It's all right, Miss.' I stroked her shoulder, very gently, and, lifting the candles around to give a better view, saw that she had a small flour sack placed over her head. This had a string gathered around the top of it which was pulled in tightly and led down to her wrists, then on to her ankles.

'You are strung up like a boiling fowl,' I said. 'Wait while I undo you.' I untied the bottom knots, released her feet, unwound the string from her hands then lifted the sack from her head. The girl who emerged was very pale, with dark copper hair the same colour as William Mucklow's must have once been. She was dressed in a dark velvet gown and cloak, and had two thick rugs about her shoulders.

'Miss Charity?' I asked, which I own was rather silly of me, for who else would it have been?

She gave a hesitant nod, screwing up her eyes at the light from the candles, and then she opened her mouth and shut it again without speaking.

'Are you all right?'

She nodded again, splayed her fingers, stretched out her arms. 'I . . . I believe so. Though I feel very . . . sleepy and confused.'

'I've come to take you home.'

She yawned and her eyes half-closed. 'I'm so tired. How long have I been down here in the dark?'

'I'm not sure. Two or three days, perhaps.'

'That long!'

'I think you were given some strong herbal preparation to send you to sleep. But do you know how you came to be here?'

She frowned. 'It was very strange. I'd escaped from my maid so that I could go for a walk without her and was enjoying the freedom, when suddenly a man on a horse stopped and presented me with a bouquet of flowers.'

'Did you see his face?'

She shook her head. 'He wore a dark riding cloak

with a hood, which was pulled forward.'

'And then?'

'Then – well, it seemed a romantic enough gesture and I thanked him kindly before bending my head to smell the bouquet. I was about to tell him that it would not be seemly for me to accept such a gift and that for certain my father wouldn't allow it, but I found the aroma of the flowers so intoxicating that it made me dizzy . . . '

'And then you swooned?' I asked, for I'd heard that the flower of the opium poppy could bring about such a thing.

'I suppose I must have done. I don't remember.' She turned to stare hard at me. 'But who are you?'

I thought it best not to answer this. 'Now, can you stand, Miss Charity?' I asked briskly. 'We must get you home.'

'Will you first lift the light to show all around us,' she asked, and this I did. 'Where's the well?' she said after a moment.

I shook my head, not knowing what she meant.

'The man said that I was poised on the edge of a bottomless well, and if I tried to escape – or even move – I'd plunge straight into it.'

'There is no well,' I said. 'You are just in a passage-way between a house and a church.'

She yawned again. 'He said that if I was quiet and good and made no sound, he'd restore me to my family quite soon.'

'So you thought it best not to shout?'

She nodded. 'I mostly kept silent – only sometimes I sighed. Of course, all the time I was wishing for someone to come and help me.'

I smiled at her. Maybe the voice had not been just my imagination, then. Maybe, somehow, I'd heard her silent call.

'I think I heard you,' I said, rubbing her ankles where the string had cut into them. 'But I must get you home to your family now. Your mother and father are frantic with worry.'

'But where are we?'

I looked at her consideringly. 'I think it's best for you not to know,' I said, 'and best for me, too. That way you can tell no one where you've been or who rescued you.'

'Whatever you wish,' she said, her eyes half-closing in sleep again.

'You must try and stand now, Miss,' I said.

Swaying slightly, holding on to me, she stood up and I fastened her cloak about her shoulders more securely, set her fur mittens on her hands and made sure her shawl was snug about her neck. She stood there patiently, allowing me to do these things as a child would, and indeed it was likely that she had always been tended and fussed over by maidservants and had never had to do them for herself.

'I'll walk home with you,' I said, 'although you must promise me faithfully that you'll try and forget the direction you're coming from.'

'I promise,' she said. 'But when I get home, what shall I tell them?'

'Tell them . . . tell them you were kept prisoner somewhere, and then you escaped – but it was fearful dark and you couldn't tell where you were. They'll be so happy to see you that they won't ask too many questions.'

'Is it very far from here?'

I shook my head. 'Not far at all.'

I was nervous about going back through the house, not only fearing that we might be heard, but that Miss Charity might recognise the house where she'd been kept prisoner. We went onwards, therefore, along the passage and soon found ourselves standing beside a ladder similar to the one I'd come down. I climbed this while my companion held the candles aloft, and, pushing open the trapdoor at the top, found, as I'd anticipated, that I was in the body of St Mary's, which was now as dark, still and cold as a burial chamber. The trapdoor through which I'd emerged was cleverly concealed between two pews, its outline hidden within the strips of old pine that made up the flooring and its ancient hinges rusted and dusty. How many worshippers, I wondered, had sat there not knowing that a secret passage lay beneath their feet?

I helped Miss Charity through, we closed the trapdoor, and then had a nervous few moments when we thought the church door might be locked from the outside. It was not, however, and we left the church-yard in the normal way through the lych-gate, only just missing the bellman on his rounds, calling three o'clock.

'Do my mother and father think I'm dead?' she asked as we walked back through the deserted lanes.

'Not dead,' I answered. 'They fear you've eloped, and have dismissed your lady's maid for her negligence!'

She laughed a little at this, and indeed sounded almost normal. 'I must find poor Susanna and reinstate her! But how can my parents think I've eloped when I've scarce spoken to a man, let alone got to know one well enough to run off with him?' She looked at me with interest. 'Do you have a sweetheart?'

I thought of Tomas straightaway. But of course he wasn't my sweetheart! 'I don't, Miss,' I said, shaking my head.

We reached the gates of Charity's father's house and I made her promise, once again, not to try and recall where she'd been.

'I will not,' she said, kissing my cheeks with great affection, 'but I will ever be grateful to you, and should a time come when I can repay your kindness in rescu-ing me, then I certainly will.'

I was embarrassed to be embraced by someone so well born, but thanked her.

'I mean it most sincerely,' she said, and she pressed her beautiful sable mittens on to me and insisted that I take them. I did so rather than be thought unmannerly, although I knew that if a maidservant appeared in such expensive finery it would be assumed that she'd stolen them. I would never wear them, I thought, nor would I ever have cause to ask for help from a lady such as she . . .

Chapter Six

I had barely one hour's sleep that night and wished I had not bothered to lay my head down at all, for I'm sure I felt the worse for it. Rising reluctantly, I went about my early morning duties in the usual way: cleaning the grates, lighting the fires, heating the washing water and simmering a pottage for Merryl and Beth's breakfast, wondering all the time what was happening at the Mucklow household and thinking how overjoyed Miss Charity's mother and father must be to have her home. My reveries about this happy scene, however, were tempered with the thought of how Dr Dee and Mr Kelly would react when they discovered that their little bird had flown the nest. How often they had checked on Miss Mucklow I didn't know, but seeing as the trapdoor to the secret passage was in such a prominent position, I thought it likely to have only been once a day – and then probably when the household was abed. If this was so, then they might not discover her disappearance until much later that night.

When I went in to light the fire in the library I had a close look about me and discovered some dried herbs in a pestle and mortar, ready for crushing. I sniffed these and thought they were the flowers of scented mayweed, which, made into an infusion, is a well-known sleeping draught. These, I supposed, together with some poppy juice, would have ensured that Charity was always too sleepy to try to escape.

It was a particularly trying morning, for Tom-fool the monkey started a high-pitched screeching which went right through our heads, this noise being accompanied by him leaping along the cupboards in the kitchen and dislodging dishes and platters. Merryl suggested that he might be feeling the cold – for there had been another very hard frost – and, thinking this the case, we found some old baby clothes and dressed him in them, which only maddened him the more, so much so that he bit me on the arm and drew blood. We shut him in the kitchen cellar as punishment for this, where he continued to squawk, scream, rattle at the latch and generally show his temper, so that when Mistress Midge announced that she had started thinking of our Christmas fare and dictated a list of provisions she needed from the market, I was only too pleased at the thought of getting out of the house.

I dressed Merryl and Beth in their warmest clothes

and we'd just set off when a maidservant wearing a thick knitted hood, bundled in shawls against the cold, came hurrying along the river path towards us.

'Can you tell me where the magician's house is?' she asked, and then gave a start of surprise. 'You are his servant, are you not?'

I nodded that I was, and when she pushed back her hood a little to reveal her face, I realised it was the maid I'd spoken to at the Mucklow house. 'You came to my master's house to deliver a letter, and now I'm bringing you the reply,' she said.

I regarded her rather warily, wondering what the letter might contain and hoping that Miss Charity had not given any hints to her father of where she'd been.

I pointed behind us. 'There. Dr Dee's house is the one we've just left.'

She brought out a parchment from under her shawl. 'Would you be good enough to take this in for me?' she asked, and added in a low voice, 'For I've heard many tales about what goes on inside that place, and to tell the truth I'm afeared to cross its threshold.'

I smiled. 'I can assure you that nothing will happen if you go in,' I said. 'You won't be changed into a Christmas goose!'

'That's what you say.' She bit her lip nervously. 'I *would* go, indeed I would, but I'm in a hurry, for my young lady's returned and there's much to do.'

'Miss Charity's back?' I asked, assuming surprise.

'She is – and because of it the whole household is set to make merry. Which is not the habitual state of affairs in a Puritan household,' she added in an undertone.

'Then she didn't elope.' I affected a look of polite enquiry. 'But where did she go?'

'Someone took her – but she says she doesn't know who, or where she was kept,' said the girl. She pulled a wry face. 'Or perhaps she did elope but didn't find the man to her liking!'

I laughed and, glancing at the letter and seeing that it bore no seal, agreed to take it in. I called the girls, telling them not to go too near the river, then hurried back into the house and along to the library, knowing that Dr Dee was not yet down. As I carried in the letter, I shook it slightly so that the topmost edge slipped out of its cut niche, the paper unfolded and the message was revealed. I own this was dishonest of me, but, having done what I had, I needed to assure myself that there was nothing in the letter which might lay the blame on me.

It was written in very plain print, was short and to the point:

Sir,

We are beholden to you for your offer to seek our daughter by magickal means and your so-called 'scrying stone'. We have to inform you, however, that by the Grace of God and without resource to witchcraft or supernatural methods she has returned to us safely.

Praise be the Name of the Lord!
I am, Sir, your servant,
William Mucklow.

I breathed out deeply, much relieved, and carefully folding the letter back into its creases, laid it on the table. I was only just in time, for as I put it down and turned towards the door I heard footsteps coming along the corridor and recognised the slow, slippered tread of Dr Dee.

My heart thumped. All was in order, but I would rather not have come face to face with him just then. He bade me the most cursory of good mornings, then, glancing at the fire to ensure it was burning as high as he liked it, asked me to remind Mistress Midge to lay in a good supply of sea-coal for the winter.

I assured him that I would. 'I'm just off to market with Beth and Merryl, Sir,' I added, hurrying towards the door. 'May I get you anything from there?'

He was about to answer me when his attention was caught by the parchment on his desk. 'What's this?'

I was so nervous that my voice caught in my throat, but I cleared it and gave a little extra cough or two, so that he'd think I merely had a winter chill. 'I believe it must be a message from Mr Mucklow,' I said, 'for one of his housemaids has just delivered it.'

Not quite a smile – for he rarely smiled – but a look of satisfaction crossed his face. 'Is the girl waiting for a reply?'

'I'm not sure, Sir.'

'Then you may have to run after her. Wait a moment, will you . . .'

I did not want to wait, but had no option other than to stand there while he unfolded the parchment. He scanned it, gave a cry and unsteadily backed himself into a chair. 'This cannot be!'

I assumed an expression of concern. 'Are you all right, Sir?'

'Fetch . . . fetch . . .'

'Some water, Sir?'

'Mr Kelly. Send a boy for Mr Kelly straightaway!'

I hurried to the kitchen to get a coin from Mistress Midge, then gave this to one of the small boys who perpetually hung around the big houses hoping to earn a halfpenny or a crust of bread, telling him to go to Mr Kelly's lodgings and request that he attend on Dr Dee with all haste.

Just a few minutes later (for he was already on his way to us, apparently) Mr Kelly arrived, whistling, full of himself, a scarlet velveteen cape swinging around his shoulders. 'He's sent the money, has he?' I heard him say to Dr Dee before he was even through the library door.

'No, he hasn't!' Dr Dee said. 'And do you ask why? Then I'll tell you: *because the girl's back with her father!*'

Well, there was no need for me to stand in the hall with my ear to the library wall, for you could hear the row that ensued as far off as the kitchen. First Mr Kelly said it couldn't be, it wasn't possible, then Dr Dee said 'the package' as he called Miss Charity, couldn't have been properly bound. This led to Mr Kelly asserting that the knots had been most carefully tied, and the correct herbs and simples administered, to which Dr Dee replied that the only other explanation was that Mr Kelly had captured the wrong package, and someone else remained below.

They went into the hall and, obviously no longer caring about being seen, lifted the trapdoor. Mr Kelly went down and when he came up (I was very nervous then, fearing I had left some means whereby I might have been discovered) he declared that she had indeed vanished, and the only explanation was that there was an evil spirit in the house who wished them ill, and who had freed the girl to thwart their plans. Hearing this I could not but smile a little to myself, grateful that they believed in the existence of such beings.

They went back into the library, still cursing, each trying to blame the other for the loss of Miss Charity.

'Well,' I said to Mistress Midge as their voices died away. 'What can all that have been about? What do you think was in that package they referred to?'

Mistress Midge was endeavouring to knead egg yolks into ground almonds and sugar to make a marchpane cake, which is a task to frustrate the most even-tempered of women. 'I don't know and Lord knows I don't care,' she said. She thumped the mixture in the bowl furiously with her knuckles, trying to get it to come together. 'Lord above! How is it that the daintiest of sweetmeats needs the heaviest of hands?'

'But didn't you hear? Dr Dee and Mr Kelly were monstrous angry with each other.'

'Not as angry as I with this!' she said, giving the mixture such a blow with her fist that the china bowl went skidding on to the floor and broke in two, depositing almond paste on to the floor. She roared with rage – and I thought it best to slip quietly away and continue my errand.

The girls and I walked beside the river into the village, discovering that the puddles along the towpath had frozen hard and that the village boys had made one into a very long slide. We queued up to use this in turn (I, too, for I was feeling very light-hearted knowing that Miss Charity was safely back home with no blame to me) and took great delight in sliding its length, occasionally ending up on our backsides with ice and frozen earth all over our clothes. There was much laughter from the village lads when this happened, for most of them had tied bundles of rags over their shoes to aid their slipping and sliding, and this made them far more able on the ice than we were. Some didn't feel the cold (or perhaps did not own any warm clothing) and did not seem to mind being hurt, either, for they were sliding and playing wearing short, ragged trousers, their legs sore and blue-mottled. All seemed to know the names of my little charges and, on Merryl falling over once again and being about to cry, set up a clapping and a chant of 'Bravo, Merryl!' until she smiled again. I was touched at this, but then heard one small boy say to his companion, 'They are the magician's children and we do well to speak to them civil.'

'And what if we don't?' came the question.

The answer was a shrug and a muttered, 'If you cross them it could be very bad.'

At length Merryl pleaded with her sister that they should go down the ice slide together, carriage-horse fashion, and crossing their arms behind them they ran two-by-two on to the ice, only to end up skidding and tumbling into a shallow ditch, laughing all the while.

Several housewives on their way to market had stopped to see the children's fun, and one of these spoke to me as I went over to help the girls out of the ditch.

'We are set for days more of this harsh weather,' she said, 'for the moon is as clear as silver in the sky a'night.'

I nodded, looking across the Thames. 'There are great chunks of ice floating in the river, and I don't believe I've ever seen their like before.'

'Nor I,' said the woman. I set Merryl upon her feet again, recrossed her shawl around her body where it had come loose and tied it at the back. 'Have you heard that near Kingston the river has almost frozen over,' the woman went on, 'and today a man is set to walk on it from one side to the other?'

'Really? He will step across on the frozen water?'

She nodded. ''Tis one of the ferrymen, and he's doing it for a bet.'

'Never!' I said. I pulled Beth from the ditch and began to rub her hands between my own to warm them.

'Aye,' said the woman. ''Tis wondrous what men will do for a silver florin, is it not?'

We both laughed. 'If he gets across, others will try it,' she said. 'There's even talk of a frost fair on the ice.'

This, we agreed, would be most exciting.

She went off towards the market and I asked the girls if they'd done enough sliding and tumbling into ditches for one day, but they pleaded for just one more slide and ran off to join the others before I could persuade them otherwise.

I was about to go to the end of the slide to wait for them when there came a voice from behind which asked sternly, 'Are those the magician's children?'

I turned to see who'd spoken so, for though I'd heard this question oft enough before, it was not usually uttered in such educated and mature tones. Looking at the speaker, however, I realised that the man in question was younger than his voice suggested, being perhaps only twenty-three or twenty-four years of age. He was tall with a neatly trimmed beard, had gingery hair under a high-brimmed hat, and was dressed like a man of fashion in doublet and padded hose, with a slashed leather jerkin atop and a cape over all.

I looked at the man and returned a frown for his frown, for I felt that this question was vulgar from one such as he. I dipped a very small curtsey. 'And who is it who asks, Sir?'

He faced me out rudely, and did not remove his hat before speaking. 'I believe it was I who put the first question.'

'That's as maybe, Sir,' I replied, 'but I don't give information about my charges to just anyone.'

He gave a short laugh. 'Your charges – yes! Yet you let them roll about in the dirt like beggars' brats. What sort of a nursemaid are you? Did your maid bring *you* up so?'

I felt my face turn red. I'd had a humble upbringing, 'twas true, but I'd never questioned whether my two girls should be raised and treated any differently from the way my ma had raised me. 'They are merely enjoying one of the few blessings of this harsh weather,' I said with some indignation. I looked him up and down. 'Maybe you are a Puritan gentleman, Sir, if you think to stop little children enjoying themselves.'

'I am not a Puritan,' he said (and indeed I already knew this from the decorated band of his hat and his brightly coloured boots). 'But if these are Dr Dee's children, then they should not be mixing with the common children of the village.'

I gave a scornful laugh. 'And who are you to say such a thing, and whether they should or no?'

There was a moment's silence before he gave a short bow and announced with some pomposity, 'I am their new tutor, Madam.'

Incredulous, I wanted to stand and gape at this, but

doing my best to act with dignity, merely said, 'Then I am your servant, Sir.'

'Yours, Madam,' he returned, before I gave the most meagre curtsey and turned away.

Without more ado, I called Beth and Merryl from the slide and we set off down the road to market. I was seething with rage, and also embarrassed and indignant. How dare he presume to tell me how to care for my own two charges!

'Why aren't you speaking to us?' Beth asked after a while, looking up at me.

'And why is your face all pink?'

'That is, it's pink where it isn't muddy!' Beth said.

'Is it muddy?' I asked crossly.

Merryl began giggling. 'Yes! You look like Tom-fool the monkey the time he got loose in the boot blacking box.'

'Oh!' I said. I got out a kerchief to scrub at my face. So I hadn't even achieved a dignified leave-taking. The children's tutor! How ever was I going to tolerate being under the same roof – and perhaps take instruction – from such a man?

Scowling, I tucked my kerchief into my pocket and set off once more, very anxious to see Isabelle and tell everything that had happened.

Chapter Seven

'**B**ring jugs of hot water!' Mr Kelly demanded when I answered the ringing of the bell in the library next morning. 'And two bowls, scissors, washing cloths and towels.'

I stared at him in surprise, wondering if he had gone a little vacant in the head. He clapped his hands. 'Now. At once.'

'As he says,' Dr Dee said, and I saw to my great surprise that Dr Dee had partly disrobed, and was standing by the fireplace wearing nothing but a loose cotton night smock.

Turning away from this alarming sight, I went to boil water and also inform Mistress Midge that the master and Mr Kelly had lost their senses. 'Either that, or they plan to set up as barber-surgeons, for they want me to bring them hot water, scissors and towels.'

'Oh, 'tis nothing but a cleansing ritual,' said

Mistress Midge. 'They do them on occasion.'

'But why?'

'It means that one of their schemes has gone awry.'

'One of their schemes . . .' I repeated. The Miss Charity one, no doubt.

'The cleansing ritual is to rid the house of any evil spirits which might have caused such a thing.'

'But why do they need washing water?'

Merryl, who was grooming Tom-fool, patiently explained, as if I were the child and she the adult: 'Father and Mr Kelly have to wash themselves thoroughly and clip their nails so that no amount of dirt is attached to their bodies. And then they must make an invocation five times to the east and five times to the west.'

'And then what?'

'Then they light brimstone, and the smoke from this drives any remaining evil spirits away from the house.'

'I see,' I said, and trusted they would never find that it was I, in fact, who had caused the collapse of their plan, and not an evil spirit at all.

The children's tutor, by name Mister Leopold Sylvester, began his tutorage of the children two days later. A small room off the hallway was designated the school room and I had been instructed to clean this and make it ready with a table, chair and stools and so on, then light a fire ready for the first lesson. You can imagine that I was extremely thorough in the dusting of this room, the washing of the window, the polishing of the table and the sweeping up and relaying of rushes on the floor. I was determined that Mr Sylvester should not discover me in any way negligent.

The fire was troublesome, however, for the chimney was unused and damp, and sent smoke into the room, and I was trying to deal with this when Dr Dee brought in Mr Sylvester to commence his lessons. Both men immediately started coughing and Dr Dee ran to throw open a window. This only made things worse, as it let icy cold air into the room and caused smoke to billow out of the fireplace in great gusts. At least this incident helped to cover the embarrassment I felt on seeing the tutor again, for by the time order was restored my cheeks had cooled. I was even able to appear unperturbed when, in response to Dr Dee's introduction, the tutor told him that we had already met. I lowered my eyes at this point, curtseyed to him very formally and said I hoped he'd find my young ladies studious and diligent in their work.

'And so do I,' he said before moving the table slightly, seating himself on the chair and taking out some books. He was dressed more in the manner of a scholar on this day, I noticed, for he wore a dark furred gown and cap and had exchanged his coloured leather boots for plain velvet slippers.

Once the fire was burning well, I took Beth and Merryl along to the school room, tapped on the door and ushered them in.

'This is Beth,' I began, propelling her forward, 'and this Merryl.'

'Good morning, young ladies,' Mr Sylvester said, inclining his head, and the girls returned his greeting and seated themselves on the stools. They were looking at him rather nervously, but this, I discovered later, was because they were fearful about what he might set them to do, not because they'd recognised him as the man on the riverbank.

I was about to leave the room, thankful that he'd not reproached me about the manner of our first meeting, when he suddenly addressed me, saying, 'Perhaps, Lucy, we should forget that we have met before and begin our acquaintance from this day.'

I looked at him, very surprised. 'Yes. Thank you, Sir.'

He nodded. 'That will be all, then,' he said, and I left the room and went back to the kitchen to report that Mr Sylvester might not, perhaps, be as niggardly a scullion as I'd first supposed.

That afternoon Mistress Midge and I were at the kitchen sink, dealing with the pots and pans from dinner, when we noticed the large numbers of people walking along the riverbank. Some of these were gathering holly and ivy for Christmastide and consequently were laden with greenery, but there were many others about, well wrapped against the weather, walking purposefully and all going the same way: upriver towards Richmond.

'It seems like a party to which everyone has been invited except us!' Beth remarked, and on the bellman going past and calling something which we didn't quite catch, she was straightaway despatched to run and ask him what he'd said. She came back to report that he was calling with news of a frost fair. 'It's on the river just before Kingston, and will be held each afternoon until the ice melts!' she added with some excitement.

'Lord above. Whatever next?' Mistress Midge muttered.

'We must go!' I responded. 'Won't you come with us?'

'To slide about on ice, to fall over and crack my head?' said that lady. 'Certainly not.'

But Merryl and Beth were fair dancing with excitement already, so I gained permission from Mistress Dee, sent them to get their warmest cloaks, boots and gloves, and we set off.

If I'd known how long the walk would take I may not have attempted the journey, but luckily I managed to get the girls a lift in a baker's handcart and walked briskly alongside them, trying to keep pace. I've said that the girls were excited, but I was equally so, for frost fairs were as rare as pig's eggs. Ma had once told me of one that she'd been to in her youth, but I'd never visited one before.

At every town and village we passed – Twickenham, Teddington, Richmond – more people joined the river walk, and all were happy, sometimes singing as they walked along, sharing slabs of gingerbread, squares of biscuit-bread or whatever victuals they had with them.

Our first glimpse of the fair came just as dusk was falling and the air was soft and misty all around. Viewed under these conditions any place can take on a kind of enchantment, but to come around the bend in the river by Hampton, to hear music playing and see the frost fair from a distance, lit at each side of the river by huge baskets of burning coals, was truly a glimpse of a kind of faeryland, and those who were on the cart jumped down and began to run along the tow path in order to reach the fair the sooner.

I'd remembered to bring some money with me, and this was soon required, for we found that the ferrymen, deprived of their usual income, had taken over the frozen river and were charging a penny for every person (and six pence for horse and carriage) to come down the bank on to the ice. Once safely down, I took Merryl and Beth by the hand and made them promise not to stray too far from me, for – perhaps attracted by the aristocracy parading the ice in their fine furs – I could see several knavish looking fellows who were no doubt out for a day's mischief and pickpocketing.

The frozen river had been smoothed over and brushed with sand to make walking easier, and between the two banks stakes had been dug into the ice, with a candle placed atop of each, so that the greater part of the fair was contained in a long, straight roadway between the two opposing riverbanks. Inside this boundary were rows of booths, some selling food-stuffs and others containing various side-shows and all the usual fun of the fair: a counting dog, a pig said to be able to speak its name, peddlers selling singing birds and pretty trifles for the ladies. Outside these confines were other activities: a sledge you could sit in and be pushed along the ice, some ponies trotting on straw, a swing-chair and a boat upon wheels, this latter with its sail outspread ready to take you along to a nearby island said to be famous for its eel pies. At another booth you could, if you were so minded, hire wooden skates which had come all the way from Holland, and a man was demonstrating these by spinning around and around in a marvellous way and attracting a large crowd.

We walked around looking at everything, at first setting down our feet gently and with some trepidation, but soon discovering that in a short while all seemed quite safe and natural and you could forget that you were walking on something so slippery.

Passing another booth, Beth gave a sudden shrill scream.

'Look down!' she instructed us. 'Look down beneath your feet!'

Merryl and I did so and shrieked as well, for where we were standing the ice had been polished clear so that one could see through it right down to the bottom of the river, where – by what miracle I couldn't say – a woman could be seen, quite dead, lying in a boat, her shroud loose and her hair floating about her.

''Tis the lady of the lake.' A knave who had been standing to one side now sprung forward. 'And you have spied her in her pretty boat coffin. That will be three pence each, if you please.'

'But we didn't *want* to see her!' I said straight, and would have liked to add that it was a river and not a lake, so how could she have been the lady of one? ''Tis only that we walked over her and there was no help for it.'

He winked at me. 'Those that see the lady of the lake find that special good fortune follows them. Nine pence, if you please.'

'But I can't afford this special good fortune!' I said, feeling in my pocket and realising that I had but ten pence in total.

'Tell you what,' he said, 'you look an honest girl. I'll do you an excellent good price – three pence for you all!'

I tried to refuse him payment, but he became so threatening that I got scared and gave him the money he asked for. Walking on quickly, I told the girls to look straight ahead and neither up, down, nor into any of the booths in case they saw something which might have to be paid for.

We each had a puff-paste biscuit, then a spiced chicken wing cooked atop of a brazier, and some warm milk fresh from the cow (for there were two such animals on the ice; their hooves well muffled with straw) and I was only surprised that I didn't see Isabelle there, selling her wares. We watched some maids dancing, fine and nimble, passed a bear-baiting and heard a ballad sung about a girl dying of love, the singer having his audience sobbing mightily by the end.

Darkness fell and, tired by now, we stopped to watch a playlet about two men in love with the same woman. There were many vulgar words spoken (or so I presumed from the coarse laughter which ensued) but I was not concerned because these were given in French. It was only when I saw Merryl and Beth giggling together that I remembered that they could speak this language, and moved them on quickly.

There was much to see, all manner of jollities, but the frozen ice under our feet at last began to chill us right through, and my thoughts turned to the journey home. Walking back to our side of the river, however, we were halted by a banner declaring: *See Jack Frost and the Merry Chimney Sweep*, and the sight of two men, one all in white and one in black, turning somersaults, each holding the other's feet and tumbling over and over.

'Is that the real Jack Frost?' Beth said in awe. 'The one that paints all the windows every morning?'

I smiled at her, nodding. 'I think it must be.'

'Is it safe to watch them perform?' Merryl whispered to me. 'Is there a charge for it?'

'It doesn't say anything . . .' I said, looking about us. I felt in my pocket: I was down to my last three pence and knew we'd need this in order to pay the ferryman's toll to get off the river. 'But we won't stay long, just in case.'

We marvelled at the two young men, who were agile indeed, turning together like a black and white wheel, circling like tops on their backs and holding each other's ankles and spinning around on the ice.

Finishing, they sprang apart and bowed to their audience, who applauded with enthusiasm and tossed coins, and Beth looked at me so reproachfully here that I dug down in my pocket again and, finding a halfpenny, gave it to her to throw. This was caught in one hand by Jack Frost, who then leapt on to a tightrope several feet above the ground and proceeded to heel-and-toe it along, as adept on a rope as he was on the ground.

When he jumped down, the merry chimney sweep took over, but he was not as clever and slipped from the rope once or twice. We watched him for a while and then began to walk to the bank, whereupon Jack Frost seemed to appear out of nowhere, springing out in front of us and making the two girls shriek with surprise.

'Madam! Is a halfpenny all we're worth?' he asked.

Seen close up, his appearance was a little frightening, for his face was a frosty-white mask dotted with glittering spangles and he wore a circlet of silver points around his head.

But I wasn't going to be cowed again, and spoke up firmly. 'I'm sure you're worth much more, Sir, but a halfpenny is all I have to spare.'

'Then you must return here another time and pay your debt!'

'I will not!' I said indignantly. I glanced down at Beth and Merryl, who were looking from one to the other of us in awe.

'Pay me . . . or have your window panes obscured by Jack Frost and his icy ferns every day of the year – aye, even in summer.'

There was something in the manner in which he said this, something about the tilt of his head and the look in his eyes . . . which were a silvery grey. 'Is it . . . ?' I asked, peering at him uncertainly. 'Are you not . . . ?'

Beth whispered something to Merryl, who whispered back, then both began laughing. ''Tis Tom-fool!' Merryl said.

I smiled, delighted. 'Tomas!'

He bowed to me, then kissed the hands of Beth and Merryl with some flourishes and a deal of ceremony, which they loved.

'What are you doing here?' I asked.

'Most of the court are here, if you know where to look.'

Hearing this, I almost forgot the long walk home. 'Are they? Then we must go and look for them, and see who we can see!' For of course I was thinking that Her Grace might have attended.

Tomas shook his head, smiling. 'She is not,' he said, seeming to understand my thoughts. 'And anyway, all the ladies are masked and in disguise.' Taking a silver coin from his pocket, he flicked it into the air for Beth to catch. 'There's a booth yonder selling hot honey—,' he began, and the girls had disappeared before he'd finished the sentence.

We looked at each other and I studied his face intently, trying to judge how he might look normally, without mask and silver spangles, for although we'd met four or five times now, he'd always been in disguise.

'You've saved me a journey,' he said in a low voice, 'for I was coming to the magician's house tomorrow to tell you that there is a mission we wish you to undertake.'

My heart quickened. 'But who is *we*?'

'Walsingham is behind all – but 'tis better that you know no other names,' he said, making me recall my similar words to Miss Charity.

'Her Grace came to visit Dr Dee and said I should accompany him to the palace over yuletide,' I told him, 'but I didn't know if this was to commence my duties to her, or merely because she found me a novelty.'

Tomas didn't enlighten me about this point. 'We will require your presence before that,' was all he said.

'And what would I have to do?' I asked eagerly.

'Merely watch and follow one of Her Grace's ladies-in-waiting.' He looked about us to ensure no one was close by. 'I will tell you briefly: she is named Madeleine Pryor and it is feared she may be involved in some plot or other, for she often disappears in the evenings when the other ladies are occupied making music together, or dancing. It seems that if ever there's something going on which will screen her movements, then she vanishes.'

'But why should that mean she's plotting?'

He shook his head. 'There are many under suspicion, and much doubt and mistrust throughout the Court at the moment, for you surely know that enemies of the queen are trying to raise an army to depose her and put the Catholic Mary Queen of Scots on to the throne of England instead.'

I nodded.

'Madeleine Pryor is Catholic also. And Walsingham gets ideas and feelings about people, which are not often wrong.'

'But I thought that if one worshipped in private, one's religious beliefs could be tolerated.'

'It's not Mistress Pryor being a follower of that religion that offends those close to the queen,' Tomas said, 'but the fact that she may be passing on information about her movements to her enemies, for as a lady-in-waiting she is privy to all that Her Grace does.'

'So I just have to watch her, and if she disappears . . .'

'. . . you must follow her. And possibly she may lead you to whoever she is consorting with.' He took my hand in his. 'You mustn't put yourself in any danger – just follow and tell us where she goes and what you see.'

I let my hand remain in his for a pleasurable moment, until modesty decreed I should remove it.

'And when should I come to the palace for this?'

'In a few days' time. The queen goes away on a private visit to her cousin in Chelsea tonight and will return to Richmond on Christmas Eve. There will be a celebration to welcome her back to Court and it's thought that in the midst of this, Mistress Pryor will take the opportunity to disappear.'

I wanted to ask a score – nay, a hundred – questions, but I could see that Beth and Merryl were already on their way back to us. 'But won't I be noticed at the palace? Won't it be seen that I'm a stranger?'

He smiled. 'Madeleine would soon notice if another of the ladies-in-waiting were set to follow her, but she won't notice you. There are nigh on a thousand or more servants at the palace, Lucy, and there will be a mighty crowd there to welcome the queen back for Christmas. You'll be able to slip in and out like a fish through waterweed.'

I nodded, fearful excited.

'And, Lucy –'

'Yes?'

'Keep your eyes and ears open at all times and tell no one what you are doing. Trust no one. No one at all.'

'Isabelle?' I asked.

'Apart from Isabelle,' he conceded, smiling.

The girls came up, yawning, their faces sticky with honey puffs, and Tomas arranged that one of the carts from the palace should take us home. A deal of people bound for Mortlake scrambled on the cart too, but we sat by the tail board where we would be able to see the frost fair until the last moment. My final, misty view of it, therefore, was of a brazier of coal burning so bright that it penetrated the gloom and, beside it, Tomas, his silver-white costume gleaming in the firelight and his halo glinting, waving to us until we turned the corner.

Chapter Eight

'A gift from the queen?' Two or three days later, on the Saturday before Christmas, I heard Merryl speaking to someone at our front door and on hearing the word *queen*, stopped what I was doing and ran up the hallway to see who it was.

'At your service, Sir,' I said to the youth who stood there. He was clearly not old enough to be addressed so, but if he came from Her Grace, he surely merited respect.

He bowed. 'I bring the queen's gift for Dr Dee,' he said, indicating a cart behind him.

My heart leapt. *Queen's gift*, I thought, and immediately visualised a chest full of treasure: gold coins, precious gems, strings of pearls and sparkling stones. I believe Merryl thought as I did, for when she looked up at me, her eyes were shining. 'We have not had one of those before,' she said.

I flung the door open wide, all the better to allow access to what I believed was forthcoming. 'Please bring it in,' I said.

The boy hesitated. 'Where d'you want it, Mistress? In the kitchen?'

I frowned slightly. 'The library would be a better place, perhaps.'

'For a haunch of venison?' he asked somewhat scornfully.

Merryl's face fell, and I believe mine did, too.

'The queen's Christmas gift to Dr Dee is a fine haunch of venison from her own hunt!' the boy said.

'The kitchen. Of course,' I said, and he went back to his cart, which I now saw was loaded with many similar items so that it stood similar to a butcher's shop, and returned with half a red deer over his shoulder.

We led him into the kitchen.

'A haunch of venison!' I announced to Mistress Midge.

She paused from pouring a kettle of boiling water over shelled almonds in order to skin them, for she was again attempting to make the marchpane cake. 'Lord above!' she said, looking at the boy drooping under the weight of it. 'How am I supposed to cook that great beastie? The turning spit has not been used for so long it has near rusted away.'

''Tis a Christmas gift from the queen,' Merryl said reproachfully.

Mistress Midge gave the side of meat a mock curtsey. 'Perhaps she will come and cook it, then,' she said.

The youth's knees were near-buckling. 'Where d'you want it?' he asked again, and we told him that he should hang it in the side passage, on one of a long row of meat-hooks.

He went away, and Merryl was asked to run and tell her father about the gift that had arrived. ''Twill send him into a fine spin,' she confided to me when the girl had gone. 'Last time he got a gift from the queen, some years back, he had to pawn half his specimens to buy her something in return.'

'And what did he buy?' I asked, for I could not imagine what one would give to a sovereign who regularly wore gold and jewels enough to sink a kingdom.

'Some articles of silver plate,' she answered. 'But Mistress Dee told me he had many sleepless nights worrying that they weren't good enough.'

I was about to ask more when Dr Dee himself ran into the kitchen, demanding to see the venison. Mistress Midge indicated it was in the passageway and he went through, where I saw him looking it up and down most respectfully, as if it showed its royal provenance. He came back into the kitchen rubbing his hands. 'We must have a grand dinner, Mistress Midge,' he said, 'at which the glorious centrepiece will be the queen's gift.'

'Oh yes, Sir?' said that lady without enthusiasm.

'We will have it cooked the old way, larded with butter and cloves and basted with claret wine and cinnamon, and serve peacock and artichoke pie alongside it, and calf's head and bacon, and soused turbot and . . .'

'I beg your pardon, Sir,' interrupted Mistress Midge, 'but who will cook and serve all these birds and beasts? Are you forgetting that we no longer have staff here, and that I am the sole cook?'

'We will hire staff!' said Dr Dee. 'We will hire cooks, gentlemen ushers to wait at table and a carver solely to slice the queen's magnificent deer.'

Mistress Midge's face began to redden, her mouth twitch. 'Very good, Sir,' was all she said.

'We will show everyone that the Dee household is still a renowned and wealthy one.'

'And when do you intend all this to take place?' she asked with barely suppressed wrath.

'Over the festive period,' replied Dr Dee, 'and the Walsinghams will be our guests.'

He swept out, but before the kitchen door had closed behind him, Mistress Midge's face had purpled and she'd gained – or seemed to have gained – a full six inches in height. She made an indescribable noise, something between a growl and a roar of fury. 'Lord above!' she shouted. 'Whatever does the man expect of me?'

Merryl and I began to move towards the door.

'As if I'm not already run into the ground with

work! As if my poor bones are not aged before their time and my legs as thin as sticks with having to constantly run hither and thither.' She paused for breath and Merryl and I slid away as silent as wraiths.

'As if my head is not wracked with pain every night thinking of all I will have to do the next day,' her voice followed us. 'As if . . .' But we had reached the peace and sanctity of the school room, where I had the dusting to do and the fire to make up ready for Mr Sylvester's arrival.

Mr Sylvester. I had feared that he might blight my position in the magician's household, but he'd done no such thing, for he'd wiped the slate clean, so to speak, that first morning, and I'd almost forgotten about the incident on the riverbank, which I'd concluded may have been due to anxiety about his forthcoming position here.

I hardly saw him: I took the girls, faces washed and hands clean, into him at ten o'clock each morning and there they stayed for two hours, receiving instruction, following which, at midday, I took in their dinner. The girls ate this alongside Mr Sylvester, who saw that they conducted themselves in a mannerly way and had also introduced them to forks, which were pronged instruments to hold down meat while cutting it. The girls had told me that the conversation which accompanied the meal was always conducted in French, as this was the language much used by lords and ladies.

Mistress Midge had quickly made use of the extra hours I now had to spare in the mornings and would ask me to run errands for her, help prepare dinner, or attend on Dr Dee and Mr Kelly, fetching and carrying them food and drink. It was on one of these occasions, going to clear a tray from the library, that I heard voices raised and, the door being ajar, paused outside in the passageway in order to hear a little more.

'This is proving impossible!' Dr Dee was saying.

'It's only impossible because you cannot discover the key,' said Mr Kelly.

Dr Dee groaned. 'I have transcribed pages of characters, letters and numbers, exactly as you have given them to me, but they mean nothing!'

'I gave them just as Madimi and Ariel dictated,' Mr Kelly said somewhat loftily. 'And – do you question the word of Ariel, the noblest of the spirits? It was Ariel who instructed Noah how to conduct himself during the Flood.'

'That may be so,' said Dr Dee. There was a pause. 'You say that Ariel points again and again to a figure of seven squares shown within a circle of light.'

'He does.'

'But what should it mean to *us*? What use are all these images – and all these letters and words written in this angelic language?'

'That is for you to discover,' said Mr Kelly dismissively. 'I don't purport to be a magician. I am just a humble scryer.'

'Yes, yes . . .'

'The medium through which the spirits speak to you.'

'But Her Grace grows impatient! The Spanish are already said to have turned a dozen brass rings into solid gold! An Italian philosopher is said to have restored three people to life with an elixir!'

'Pish!' Mr Kelly said. 'The Spanish are counterfeiting. 'Tis nothing but sleight of hand – a conjurer's trick.'

'Nevertheless, the Spanish court is buzzing with the story.'

'If we had the money to buy a dozen gold rings, Dee, then we could do such things.'

'But we have not the money! There is none to spare, and I already have to buy a New Year present for the queen.'

I heard Mr Kelly rise and begin to walk about the room. 'If our earlier plan had succeeded . . . if there had not been an evil spirit in the house who wished us ill.'

'Quite! But 'tis damned strange, Kelly, that a spirit should be capable of . . .'

As soon as I heard where his sentence was heading, I thought it best to go in, for if they began to reason between them what a spirit might or might not do and whether it could have released Miss Charity, then they might come to the conclusion that only someone on earth, someone human, could have caused their prisoner to escape.

* * *

A thaw had set in over the last couple of days and we'd heard that, following someone falling through a patch of thin ice at the frost fair and being drowned, it had been dismantled. No one knew, of course, when there might be such an entertainment again, for this was so dependent on the weather, and I counted myself extreme lucky to have been able to attend.

One afternoon Mistress Midge asked me to take the girls out to collect greenery for the house for, the Walsinghams having been invited to dine on the day after Christmas, Dr Dee was demanding that the house should look as fine and as festive as possible. Mistress Midge sniffed mightily at this. 'The Walsinghams are used to dining at Whitehall, at Windsor Castle and Syon,' she said. 'What sort of show can *we* ever hope to put on?'

Nevertheless, an old handcart was found in one of the outhouses and, with Merryl and Beth sitting atop, I set for Barnes Common, which I'd been assured was replete with holly, ivy and fir. Here I quickly filled the cart to capacity with all sorts of berried and evergreen branches, cutting and chopping and getting mightily scratched along the way.

On the way back, knowing that Isabelle lived nearby, I called at her little cottage on the chance that she'd be in. Her mother came to the door, however, to say that Isabelle and her sister were on the common engaged on the same errand as I, so I thanked her and didn't ask to wait. I could see by the way she stood to prevent me seeing inside that she was embarrassed about the humbleness of the cottage, which was very bare and had little in the way of furnishings or comfort. Isabelle had told me that there was never any money to spend on such things, for there were five children and no father to provide for them.

Happily, however, we three met up with Isabelle and Margaret, their shawls full of great amounts of mistletoe, as we trundled back over the common towards the river path. We stopped and spoke for a while and I told her a little about the mission that Tomas had given me.

'You are to go to the palace?' she gasped. 'To an entertainment?'

I nodded. 'And I'm excited and afeared equally.'

'But whatever will you wear?'

I stared at her in consternation, for I hadn't had a moment to consider this. 'My pale green linen, I suppose.'

'*That?!*'

'Is it not grand enough?'

She shook her head. 'I should say not.'

'The grey wool?'

'Never!'

I was stumped then, for although I had two kirtles and bodices of my own – and two gowns which had been given to me by Mistress Dee – they were all fearfully out of fashion and, now I thought of it, of course were not at all suitable for a grand occasion.

'But does it matter?' I asked. 'No one will notice me. Or if they do, they'll just suppose me to be a lady's maid.'

'Even ladies' maids dress like ladies – especially if they're going to the palace,' she said. 'You'll only slip into the background if you're dressed as fine and fashionable as everyone else. If you're dressed like a drab, then you'll stand out and people will wonder who you are and how you come to be there.'

I sighed, thinking that possibly she was right.

'We must try and think of something else for you to wear.' Her eyes suddenly sparkled. 'But now tell me of the frost fair, for I was monstrous sorry to have missed it.'

'Indeed! I felt sure I'd see you there.'

'I had no time. I've been working every day these five days past, making kissing boughs and selling them at market.'

'Have you done well?'

'I have. I've sold so many that we are to have a roast goose for Christmas Day – and I've already picked him out!'

'Kissing boughs . . .' I mused. 'Perhaps we should have one such in the magician's house, for the Walsinghams are coming and Dr Dee wants everything to look very fine.'

'The Walsinghams!' she said, impressed. She smiled. 'But did you know that if a man catches you under the mistletoe bough, then he can claim a kiss?'

I nodded, for this was an old tradition.

'Then perhaps there will be a young male Walsingham who is comely and catches your eye . . .'

I shook my head, smiling. 'Their children are all too young. Besides, any young sir would not look at me!'

'The girls' tutor, then?'

'Never!'

'Dr Dee himself?'

I screamed.

'Then, perhaps . . . Tomas, the queen's fool?'

I laughed. 'Perhaps! But what of you? Which young man will you be lingering under the mistletoe for?'

'I think . . . the 'prentice boy at the butcher's,' she said. 'For he has a fine head of red hair and always winks at me when I go in the shop.'

I laughed. 'A butcher's 'prentice?' I said. 'Are you sure that you're not just after his pigs' trotters?' And we both giggled immoderately at this.

Isabelle gave me an amount of mistletoe, saying I'd not be able to get any for myself for, it being only found atop of trees, her little sister had had to climb for it, and she showed me how to make a kissing bough by twisting it around and about with strands of vine and making it into a globe shape, then balancing a candlestick inside. 'You must hang it in the hallway, and for every kiss given, you must take off a berry,' she informed me.

I nodded. 'And after Twelfth Night, we will count our berries and see who has the most!'

We bade each other goodbye, and Beth, Merryl and I set off across the common for home (with me pondering all the way about what I should wear to the palace) and reached the river path just as dusk was falling. It was only a short walk back to Mortlake but was made harder by the unevenness of the ground and the cart I had to push, so I was happy to see the magician's house come into sight around the bend of the river. As it did so, Beth clapped her hands delightedly, saying, 'Jack Frost!'

'Really?' I asked. 'Where?'

'Standing behind that tree,' Merryl pointed to a willow on the bank. 'Ready to come around the house and paint our windows white.'

And indeed it was he and I found a smile coming to my face and my heart giving a skip, for I couldn't help thinking of all the mistletoe on my cart.

The girls ran up to him. 'Will you do a somersault for us?' Beth asked.

'No, I want you to spin round and round like a top!' Merryl commanded.

'Stop!' I said to the girls. 'Even the queen's fool is entitled to have some time off.'

'I would speak with you alone,' he said to me. His voice was low, throaty, and he put his hand to his mouth as he spoke.

'Are you well?' I asked, concerned.

'No . . . you must excuse me . . . I have an ague.'

'That such as Jack Frost should take chill! Shame!' I said.

But he didn't continue with the jest and, feeling a little perplexed at this, I sent the girls indoors saying I'd follow directly.

'What is it?' I asked. 'Why have you come?'

'Have you anything to tell me?'

I shook my head, not knowing what he meant.

'You have to watch someone . . .'

'Yes,' I said, puzzled.

'Can you recall the name of this person?'

'Of course,' I said straight, thinking this some testing of my sense or my memory.

'Are you sure?'

I nodded assuredly.

'And that name is . . . ?'

I was about to blurt out the name Madeleine Pryor when I heard a voice inside my head, a voice clearly telling me not to reply, and I looked more closely at the white mask of Jack Frost . . . through the eyeholes to the eyes underneath . . . *which were not grey, but brown.*

'Come, Mistress, have you forgotten?' he said briskly.

'I have not.'

'Then tell me.'

I put out my hand and would have snatched off his mask, but he judged what I was about to do and stepped back. 'You are not Tomas!'

He tried to make light of it. 'No, indeed, I am Jack Frost.'

'You are not he, either!' I said. I wheeled around

and, taking hold of the handles of my cart, would have pushed it into him, except that he sprang away from me and I heard his laughter echoing down the empty riverbank as he ran off.

Chapter Nine

At the frost fair Tomas had told me to trust no one, but I'd hardly heeded his words. I would from now on, however, for clearly someone had seen him speaking to me – someone who knew that he was not only the queen's fool, but also acted as her emissary, and thus had reasoned that I'd been asked to engage in some secret work. Realising all this, I would have written to Tomas to inform him, except that I had no parchment nor quill. Besides, I realised, if I was being watched, any letter might be taken straight to the counterfeit Tomas.

I did nothing, therefore, but used what little leisure time I had in the worry of what I was going to wear to the palace and how I was going to behave while I was there, for I had begun to fear that I might show myself up through not knowing what was mannerly. I didn't know what the entertainments at the palace might consist of: music, dancing, a masquerade, mummers singing Christmas songs? Even, perhaps, jousting in the tiltyard. Each of these would demand a different response from the onlookers and, the Court being so conservative in its customs and etiquette, I had next to no idea of what this response might be.

That evening, when the girls had gone to bed, I laid all my clothes – bodices, kirtles, sleeves and smocks – on my bed, held my candlestick high and scrutinised them for some time, unhappily coming to the same conclusion as Isabelle: nothing I owned was in any way suitable to wear to an entertainment in front of the queen at Richmond Palace. The style of the kirtles – and the necklines, lacing, embroidery, bodices and ruffs, too – was dated, the fabric dull and faded, and those items of clothing that were not darned had either grease spots or marks around the hems where I'd endeavoured to brush away the winter's mud. I looked at them, and then I thought about the queen's ladies-in-waiting and maids of honour, those bright young women who acted as an attractive and elegant back-drop for Her Grace, and sighed heavily. I'd been to the palace before, that was true, and had not worried about my gown to that extent, but then I'd just been one of a couple of hundred other ordinary citizens seeking an audience in the presence chamber. This time I was actually going to be part of the Court.

My eyes fell on the only costly and fashionable thing I owned: the sable mittens given to me by Miss Charity, and I suddenly remembered how grateful she'd been to me. She'd told me I must go to her if I ever wanted anything. Had she meant what she'd said?

There was, I thought, only one way to find out.

'Good morning,' I said politely when Thomas Mucklow's front door was opened the next morning.

The housemaid – who was not the one I'd met previously – looked me up and down. 'Trades at the back door,' she said.

I felt my face turn pink. 'I am not *trades*,' I said. 'I've come to speak with Miss Charity.'

'Have you indeed?'

I stood my ground. 'Would you kindly tell her that a friend . . .'

As I said this last word, she smirked.

'A *friend*,' I said firmly, 'wishes to speak to her.'

'And who is this person? This friend?' asked the housemaid.

'My name is Mistress Mary Ditcham,' I said, making up the name on the spot. I hoped that Miss Charity would remember me, but I'd bought her mittens along to jog her memory, just in case she didn't.

'I've not heard of no one of that name.'

'Nevertheless, I am she. I am a friend of Miss Charity's and bring something belonging to her,' I said, indicating the package under my arm.

'Very well,' said the maid sullenly. 'I'll tell her.' She left me standing at the door, went up the facing flight of stairs and knocked on a door. I heard her say, 'A person has called who says she is your friend, Miss, but I think it might be someone from the market trying to sell you something.'

After a moment Miss Charity came down the stairs on her own. She was dressed very neat and pretty in a deep red gown embroidered with gold leaves and flowers, her auburn hair caught into a gold net studded all over with tiny red stones. She looked at me hesitantly for a moment, and I brought out the package. 'Your mittens, Miss,' I said.

Her face cleared. 'Oh! What shall I call you?' she asked in a whisper.

'Mistress Mary Ditcham, if it please you, Madam,' I whispered back.

'Do come upstairs, Mary,' she said, and she led me into a long bedchamber at the front of the building. This, I saw immediately, had not been furnished on Puritan principles like the rest of the gloomy house, but was very light and pretty, with a four-post bed hung around with light draperies and two wood benches having coloured velvet cushions. The wall hangings, too, were not improving stories from the Bible, but gaily coloured pastoral scenes on painted silk, with maidens and lambs frolicking in fields, or lovers walking together through flowery meadows.

'I suppose that Mistress Ditcham isn't your real name?' my young lady asked.

I shook my head.

'Very sensible.'

I hesitated. 'I hope you'll forgive my boldness in coming to see you, Miss, but . . .'

'You must call me Charity if we're supposed to be friends!'

'Charity,' I ventured, 'you said that I was to approach you if ever I needed anything.'

'I did indeed. And I meant it.'

'I trust you have suffered no harm as a result of what happened to you?'

'I can barely remember it!'

I nodded. 'I daresay that is because of the poppy juice.'

'But do tell me more, because I'm most intrigued as to why you're here.'

I took a deep breath. 'Well, here it is as plain as flour, Mi— . . . Charity. I have to go somewhere very important on Christmas Eve.'

'Do you?' she asked, and sighed. 'Is it a dance or a ball? I wish very much that I could hold a dance, but father has banned any form of gaiety from the house this Yuletide.'

I looked at her with sympathy.

'But I'm sorry I interrupted. Do go on!'

'You see, I haven't got anything suitable to wear to this important place, only my everyday gowns, which – now that I've looked at them closely – are very dull and horrid.'

'And you'd like me to give you something?'

'Not give, Miss,' I said, mortified that she'd presume such a thing. 'If I could just borrow a gown from you 'twould be more than enough.'

'No, indeed you cannot.'

'Oh!' I said, saddened and worried that I had offended her by asking for too much.

'But I'll *give* you a gown – for heaven knows I have enough, and nowhere to wear them. Moreover, I insist that you have two gowns, so that if you get invited somewhere else then you'll have something different to wear, which is only seemly.'

When I tried to protest, she would have none of it, and simply said, 'In return you must come to see me and tell me about the occasion, of how you looked and how everyone else looked.'

'If you wish,' I said, 'of course I will.'

'For you cannot know how much I long to go into society!'

'And your father won't allow you?'

She shook her head. 'He believes that the world is full of sin and treachery and at any time I might fall into the devil's hands.'

I thought about this. 'You nearly *did* fall . . .'

'But you rescued me!'

She went into a small room, which I supposed was her dressing room, for it had a pitcher and bowl for washing, a padded night stool and a long shelf containing hats and hoods, various hair decorations, false topknots of curls and so on. Hanging all around

squares of gold leaf, so that it looked very fine and festive.

'I've been thinking long about the cooking of the venison,' she said, 'and have obtained an excellent recipe from my sister for a gallendine sauce to garnish it. 'Tis a *royal* method she has told me, made with claret wine, cinnamon, ginger, cloves and sugar.' She winked at me. 'It will show the Walsinghams that the Dee family are served by a very skilled and most knowledgeable cook!'

As she was so gay, I took the opportunity to ask if I might, once Merryl and Beth were in bed, go a-mumming around the houses with Isabelle and her sisters (for I did not, of course, intend to tell her I was going to the palace).

'You may,' she said. 'I did the same in my youth and 'tis an excellent way to get a few coins in your pocket.' And, rolling out a yard of pastry, she sang,

'A jug of Christmas ale, Sir, will make our voices ring,
Money in our pockets is a very good thing!'

I laughed and we sang this again, together, and a moment later a smiling Mr Sylvester (for he had heard us for sure) put his head around the door and said that the fire was very low in the school room and could it be made up.

I went in with a pail of coal and, feeling confident of the answer, paused to ask if Merryl and Beth were doing well at their studies.

'Indeed, they are very diligent,' said Mr Sylvester. He

wore a schoolmaster's gown as usual, but underneath I was surprised to see a heavily decorated jerkin and embroidered shirt – more the clothes of a court dandy.

Beth stopped writing and smiled up at me, pleased to be praised, and I looked to see what she was copying from her horn book.

'Do you read?' Mr Sylvester asked in a startled voice.

I was torn here, on the one hand wanting to continue the impression of being a simple housemaid, on the other not wishing to appear ignorant in front of such a clever and personable man.

'A . . . a little,' I said. 'But that is merely through the girls' attentions to me, for before you came they had taught me to read and write my name, and we would often play word games together.'

He was clearly surprised, but didn't say so and, bending over Beth's horn book once more, I saw that it bore a kind of map of all the kings of our country: mostly having the names of John, Henry and Richard.

''Tis called a family tree,' Mr Sylvester said. ''Tis so that one can see the provenance of our monarchs.'

My fingers touched the one right at the bottom. 'Elizabeth,' I read out.

'That's right. And we have just been learning – have we not, Beth and Merryl? – of the queen's position and the tale of how she came to reign over us.'

'Her mother's head was cut off!' Beth said, and I blushed, for although everyone knew about this beheading, of course, it was not seemly – indeed was thought almost treasonous – to speak of it in public.

'Her mother was Anne Boleyn and she was the second wife of Henry,' Merryl recounted. 'And her brother Edward reigned first, and after he died, her half-sister Mary Tudor took the throne.'

'Correct,' said Mr Sylvester, nodding.

'But lots of people say that her cousin, Mary Stuart, the Queen of Scotland, should rule England,' said Beth in a very forthright manner.

'Hush!' I said, shocked. I appealed to her tutor. 'She must not speak such things aloud, must she?'

He didn't reply for a moment, but I watched a tiny nerve tick in his jaw. 'Everyone should be free to say what they think within their own walls.'

'But . . .'

'Mary Stuart's followers title her Queen of England as well as Scotland,' he said. 'Whether or not one agrees with this, it's as well to know the facts.'

I hesitated a moment, then said, 'What are the facts?' For although Tomas had spoken of the matter, and I sometimes overheard people talking about it in the marketplace, I did not know the particulars, or what lay behind it all. 'Why should Mary, Queen of Scots, seek to take our throne?' I asked somewhat indignantly.

Mr Sylvester stood up and looked out of the window. 'At the hour of Mary Tudor's death there were many who believed that Mary Stuart was the true Queen of England, and should rule forthwith.'

I gasped at this, for I'd never heard it spoken so boldly before. 'Why is this?'

'Why? Because some people – the Catholics – hold that the marriage of our queen's father and mother was invalid, for King Henry was previously married to Queen Katherine of Aragon before Anne Boleyn, and of course the old church does not recognise divorce.'

I still didn't really understand.

'If their marriage was not a true one,' he explained, seeing my puzzled face, 'then it follows that any child of that marriage – by this I mean our good queen – is illegitimate, and therefore barred from the throne of England.'

I could not utter a word, so appalled was I at this treason.

'Mary Stuart of Scotland is cousin to our queen,' he said. 'They are granddaughters of the seventh Henry, therefore both have an equal claim to the throne – or at least, that's what some people think.' He paused and added, 'And of course Mary Stuart has no stain of illegitimacy over her.'

I was filled with sudden horror. 'But, Sir!' I said. 'Surely God alone decides who should be on the throne of England? He has already chosen Elizabeth and 'tis she who reigns over us.'

He turned away from the window and regarded me steadily. 'Yes, that's correct. He has and she does.'

'He has decreed that Elizabeth should be our sovereign lady,' I went on fervently, 'and surely there cannot be a better queen than Her Grace, for she has proved to be good and wise, and loves her subjects dearly.'

He nodded and resumed his seat at the table. 'Indeed! Everything you say is correct.'

'Then – and excuse my talking to you so forthright, Sir – please speak no more about those wicked people who seek to put another queen in her place.'

He smiled a little at this. 'But you wished to know the facts. And it is always wise to know the other point of view.'

'But now I know, I want to hear no more,' I said firmly. 'May God save our good queen and long to reign over us!'

'God save the queen!' echoed Beth and Merryl in unison, and Mr Sylvester said, 'Amen to that.'

I bobbed him a curtsey. 'I'll bring your dinner in directly, Sir,' I said, and went back to the kitchen to lay up a tray with trenchers and spoons.

In spite of my earlier gaiety, however, and even in spite of having two new gowns hanging up in my chamber, I felt ill at ease. Tomas had told me to trust no one. Did that warning also apply to members of the Dee household? What if Mr Sylvester was a supporter of Scotland's queen and had taken the role of tutor at her magician's house in order to be in close proximity to Her Grace? What if he meant her harm?

Or were such thoughts, I mused, the result of an overheated and over-curious mind?

Chapter Ten

The following morning, finishing my usual chores early and the girls being with Mr Sylvester, I sought out Mistress Midge to ask which rooms I should decorate with greenery in readiness for Christmas Day. I found her in the kitchen as usual, standing at the window and gossiping with a neighbour on her way back from market.

She was there for some time but, at last, the woman going off, she banged the window shut and turned to me, her solid, ruddy face looking worried. 'Mistress Utting says there's plague at Putney.'

'Not so!' I searched my mind for the last time I'd heard of anyone having plague: probably four or more years back, at home. 'But it's midwinter! Doesn't plague only strike in the summer months?'

'That's just it. Because it's not usual at this time of year the authorities are putting it about that it's spotted fever.'

'Then maybe it is.'

She shook her head. 'Mistress Utting says everyone thinks it's plague, and it's been entered so in the parish notices.'

'Is it contained at Putney?'

She shrugged. 'It's said to be in just one house, but who knows? The pestilence travels . . . At any minute it could jump on to a barge and land up at Mortlake wharf, and then where would we be?' I didn't reply to this and she answered, 'Dead within minutes. And it will strike the weak and overworked first!'

I braced myself here, fearing that the word *overworked* would bring with it an avalanche of complaints against the Dee family, but she merely sniffed and carried on with what she was doing, which was making pastry for a taffety tart ready for the Walsinghams' visit on the day after Christmas.

'Well, now, let me think,' she said when I asked about Yuletide decorations. She was holding a tin aloft, as big as a wheel, and cutting off the spare pastry all round it. 'It's some years since we brought in the green. At one time the house was always decorated, but that was when we had more servants. Once it was down to me – well, I couldn't manage to do that along with everything else.'

'Certainly you couldn't,' I agreed quickly.

She delved into a drum of last summer's apples, pulled one out and began peeling it. 'But start with the dining room,' she said, 'for that room at least must be gay for our visitors.'

'And then I'll pin ivy along the hallway,' I said, 'and in the school room, and in here, too, so that we can enjoy it.'

''Twill shrivel too quickly in the heat here and never last twelve days!'

'Then when it fades, I'll put up fresh,' I said. 'Should I decorate the library, too?'

'You must ask the master about that.'

'And what about in the mistress's rooms?'

She sniffed. ''Twould take more than a few springs of holly to bring cheer to those upstairs,' she said. 'I can't remember when I last saw Mistress Allen crack her cheeks in a smile.'

She finished peeling an apple, threw the peel over her left shoulder and looked to see what initial it had made. 'It's a C,' she sniffed. 'It always comes to a C, and that suits me well, for I don't know anyone of that name and wouldn't marry them anyway.'

Laughing at this, I peeled an apple in one strip and tried for myself, but the peel broke into three pieces as it landed and didn't make any initial at all.

To my surprise, Dr Dee said he would like holly and ivy put about the library.

''Twas once considered a pagan custom to decorate with evergreens, but 'tis done everywhere now,' he said. 'And we must have a Yule log. Tell Mistress Midge to arrange that with Mr Gibbs the woodman, will you?'

'Yes, Sir,' I said, hiding my surprise at this long speech to me, for he never spoke ten words where one would do.

'We must have everything in place and all very fine for the Walsinghams' dinner.'

I lay streamers of dark green ivy along the library mantelpieces and sprigs of berried holly along the bookshelves, but did not decorate any of his specimens, still being slightly apprehensive of both the skull and of a great stuffed bird with hooked beak. I'd just begun to fill the two great porcelain vases beside the central fireplace with holly and fir branches when Mistress Dee, still in her night attire, came into the library on the arm of Mistress Allen. Her companion settled her on to a stool, placed a rug over her knees and then went away.

Although I was at the far end of the room I could clearly hear the conversation which then ensued between my master and mistress, which centred around what they should buy the queen for her New Year gift.

'My dear, she has given us a fine present and will expect that it is reciprocated,' Dr Dee said. 'We must give her something precious. A jewelled fan, a treasure box, a diamond bracelet...'

'But she knows we're not wealthy. You're a mathematician, John, not a rich courtier. We don't have the resources to buy such precious things.'

'Nevertheless, she *will* expect it. I have already

heard that Robert Dudley is buying her a jewelled clock for her wrist.'

'A clock for her wrist? How can that be?'

''Tis in miniature. 'Twill have a little door on it which can be opened and the time seen.'

'Marvellous!' Mistress Dee exclaimed.

'And Sir Francis Drake is having a lion made all in diamonds, which will sit inside a silver cage.'

'My dear—'

'She will expect something good from us in return for the venison,' Dr Dee said resolutely. 'She will think ill of it if we merely send our good wishes. She will be insulted!'

'Then are you saying we must bankrupt ourselves to buy some frippery? Some dainty gee-gaw which she may never use?'

'Yes,' came the firm reply.

Mistress Dee gave a cry of exasperation and I looked through my greenery to see her casting the rug to one side and making for the door. I was very astonished at this, for she was ever the acquiescent, dutiful wife, but was not surprised at Dr Dee, for though my experience of Court had so far been brief, I knew that men were prepared to give their very souls if they thought a certain gift would gain them a place in the queen's circle of intimates.

The vases held a considerable amount of green-stuffs, so much so that I had to go back to the outhouse to get more, and in the midst of my arrangements Mr

Kelly arrived, demanding hot spiced wine and bread to sop in it, so I had to leave my vases to get what he wanted. Returning to the library I heard them once again speaking of the queen's New Year gift, so I surmised that Mr Kelly had been told of Dr Dee's earlier discussion with his wife.

I put down the tray containing the items I'd prepared for Mr Kelly, then went to the other end of the room and, pretending discontent with what I'd done, pulled the fir branches and the holly on to the floor to start again. A spy, Tomas had told me, should have eyes and ears everywhere and at all times.

The two men spoke of the various devices, of the jewels, gowns and costly novelties which had been presented to Her Grace over the past years, then Dr Dee rose and circled the table on which was set the alembic; the distilling equipment which, though now silent, usually contained an amount of liquid bubbling and pulsing along its tubes and channels. 'If we could only discover the precious stone,' he said longingly. 'If only we could give the queen the gift her heart really desires. How we would be raised up then, Kelly!'

'If only the moon were blue, Dee,' returned the other man.

'But other philosophers have had some success. In Prague, they say, a length of wire has been transmuted to pure gold. And in France they speak of an elixir which turned an old man's white hair dark, and gave him the stamina of a twenty year old.'

'Then, sadly, our angels cannot care enough for us,' said Mr Kelly, 'or they would give us the formula in a language we understand and thus make us rich.'

'Ah,' sighed Dr Dee.

There was a pause in their conversation and I carried on busily moving stems of holly around the vases, although it seemed that they had forgotten about me.

'Of course . . . there is a way whereby two problems may be solved at once,' Mr Kelly said.

Dr Dee turned away, raising his hand as if to block out Mr Kelly's next words. 'Talk no more of devious deeds.'

'No, no, hear me out! The first problem is the queen's New Year present, and the second is knowing what amusement or experiment we should put before her and her Court when we attend the palace. Do I speak true?'

'You do,' said Dr Dee.

'Then what if these problems were combined – and solved – together?'

'How so?'

'What if part of the entertainment we present was the mystical turning of a metal ring into a gold one, which could then be presented to the queen as a New Year gift?'

'But we are not able to perform such a task! 'Tis impossible.'

I think a look passed between them, for there was a

long pause. 'Are you suggesting that we carry out a *deception*?' Dr Dee asked.

'Of course,' said Mr Kelly easily. 'It can be simply done. We will set up the alembic in the presence of the Court and cause a little smoke and a little steam. We will utilise the dark mirror, and the onlookers will be so fascinated by this wonder of magick and science combined that a sleight of hand will go unnoticed.'

'You intend to substitute one ring for another?'

'Exactly.' Mr Kelly suddenly gestured towards me and I hastily lowered my head. 'We have to take the girl to the palace, do we not?'

'So Her Grace has requested.'

'Well then, Dee. She can be the bearer of the gold ring and the disposer of the metal one, thus leaving our hands clean. The matter couldn't be easier.'

'But . . . but what if we are found out?'

'If we are found out, Dee, then it hardly matters. We are there as an entertainment, nothing more. Besides, most of the court will be drunk on a combination of Rhenish and their own self-importance. They are so intent on making an impression on everyone else that they won't care about us.'

Dr Dee shook his head. 'I don't know. I don't know . . .'

Silence ensued, and both, staring idly down the room, looked straight at me. I had finished my arranging by then and I had no legitimate reason for staying there, so put the filled vases in position each side of the centre fireplace, threw some holly cuttings on the fire, curtseyed and went out.

It would all happen as Mr Kelly had suggested, of that I was sure. Dr Dee was the wiser of the two, but he was old and gullible and liked to please Mr Kelly, for *he* was the one who relayed the words of the angels. Or said he did.

Going back into the kitchen I found Mistress Allen giving specific directions to Mistress Midge for the making of a posset to cure Madam's lethargy. Mistress Midge managed to contain herself until the other left, then exploded in a riot of indignation.

'As if I don't know what the mistress wants and needs! As if I wouldn't know the cause and the cure of every ill she had. I, who helped birth her and breathe life into her! Three drops of this, she says, four pinches of that, six spoonfuls of the other – telling me my job! *I'm* the cook here and I'll decide what goes into Madam's posset!'

She paused for breath.

'Of course,' I agreed quickly.

'And do you know what else?'

I shook my head.

'She tried to tell me how to cook the venison!'

I made exasperated noises and soothing noises, and when she calmed down I got her to help me form the kissing bough with some vines and evergreen, bent and tied with string into a circle, with mistletoe twirled around and a candlestick fixed inside. We fastened this over the entrance to the outside passageway, so that anyone entering had to pass under it, and it looked very pretty there. It set me thinking of home, for one year my elder sister had made one, and we'd all had fun – even Ma – telling the names of those we'd like to meet underneath it, and those we'd run a mile to avoid. Sadly it had not stayed up more than a day, however, for my father, coming home drunk from the tavern that night, had hit his head on it. It could not have been a hard blow, for the bough was light and flimsy, but it was enough to enrage him, and, roaring with anger, he'd pulled down the device and kicked it into the street.

Thinking of home, I couldn't decide if I was happy to be away from it because of my father, or sad because I missed my ma. And then I forgot all this in the excitement of recalling that the following day was Christmas Eve and I was going to be at Richmond Palace.

Chapter Eleven

I'm afraid that my little charges went to bed rather early the next evening, for I had much to do to make myself ready. Isabelle came to the house to help me with this and, after I'd washed my hair and dried it before the fire, endeavoured to braid it for me. Being clean meant it was limp, however, and it kept slipping out from its braids, so – fancy hair being unattainable – all I could do was pull it straight back from my face, twist the length of it around my hand and tie it in a knot. Isabelle then gave me two black-tipped hairpins from her own hair and I put these through the knot to secure it.

'Will it do?' I asked her, turning this way and that. 'Is it grand enough?'

'It suits you mightily,' she assured me. 'And I've brought something for you to use on your face.'

'Some ceruse?' I asked, for this was how the queen

and her ladies whitened their faces.

She shook her head. 'Something I was given at market: a muslin cloth dipped in rosemary and lavender oil. The seller assured me it would lighten the complexion and make it fair and beautiful.'

'What do I have to do to make it work?'

'Merely wipe it across your cheeks and forehead.'

I carefully did so then turned to face her. 'Now. Do I look different?'

She started backwards, pretending shock, and we fell to laughing.

I'd decided to wear the pale blue gown, as it had brushed cotton petticoats, and was probably the warmer, for if everyone had to stay outside for some time while greeting the queen, then it might get very cold.

My dressing took some time. Although the vast skirts did not require me to wear a farthingale with whale-bone cage underneath, they did have to be elevated and widened by a bum roll. Isabelle tied this around me, saw that the padding was even back and front, then laced the stiffened underbodice into place, wound me into the underskirt and finally pinned me into the kirtle. After securing the top of the gown to the bottom she began fastening the scores of tiny buttons which went all down the back of it and, this done, pinned on the sleeves, crawled under the skirts to make them stand proud and finally stood back and admired me.

'How do I look?' I asked anxiously. 'Will I pass for a lady?'

She nodded keenly. 'You look very fine! You'll be kissed under the mistle-bough for sure.'

'I'm not going there to be kissed!' I said, pretending severity. 'I'm going to follow someone who may seek to harm our lady queen.' I shivered and added, 'And I hope I run into no harm.'

'I'm sure you will not. After all, you have something to guide you.'

I looked at her, puzzled. 'What do you mean?'

She shrugged. 'Well, you say 'tis not the Sight, but I believe it is something very like, something which will warn you of any danger – as it did before when Her Grace was in peril.'

I nodded slowly. 'But let's talk about other things,' I said, for it made me uneasy to think I might have mystical powers like those of witches. 'Did you hear that Robert Dudley is said to be giving the queen a little jewelled clock for her wrist?'

She nodded. 'Which will surely drive her French suitor to give her an even more precious gift.' She looked at me excitedly. 'You may see all her men tonight.'

I nodded. 'And I will certainly see Tomas.'

She paused over the task she was at, which was picking dropped pins from the floor. 'It's very strange, is it not, that you've never seen him out of disguise?'

'It is. But in public he most often appears so.'

'Why's that?'

I turned a little, trying to see my reflection in the window. 'So that, unseen and unknown, he may carry out certain duties for Her Grace. If people knew that the queen's fool was amongst them then they wouldn't speak freely.'

'Are his features good, do you think? Is he handsome?'

I smiled. 'As far as I can tell.'

'Today I served a woman in the market who wore a full veil,' Isabelle said thoughtfully. 'I thought she was dressed this way because she was in mourning, but when the wind blew her veil across I saw that she'd been badly ravaged by smallpox and her face was covered with pitting and scars.'

'Poor woman,' I gasped.

'Not that I'm saying Tomas is marked so!' she added hastily. 'For I saw a goodly part of his features when we were at the palace and I saw nothing untoward.' She stood up and took my hand. 'Come. I'll walk with you through Barnes and see you on the road to the palace.'

I smiled at her gratefully. 'And if you see Mistress Midge on our way out, remember that we are supposed to be going a-mumming.'

Isabelle looked at me and raised her eyebrows. 'A finer-dressed mummer she will never have seen in all her life!'

* * *

It was obvious to me that Tomas, Sir Francis Walsingham and whoever else had decided I should visit the palace to spy on Mistress Pryor had not given a thought as to how I might get from Mortlake to Richmond. Such a thing wouldn't have occurred, for they, being of some import, would either ride to places on horseback or be driven there in carriages. It fell to me, however, to make my way on foot, which meant wearing pattens over my shoes and holding my skirts as high as possible to keep them out of the mud.

After leaving Isabelle, I paid a penny to a link-boy to light my way on, but after crossing the deer park, I found myself at Richmond Hill and here dismissed him because light was now provided by both the newly-risen moon and the torches which flamed outside the grand houses (and he was demanding another penny). Reaching the brow of the hill, I paused, gazing at the sublime view of the moon reflected in the twisting Thames far below. On the right, Richmond Palace was lit up with so many torches and candles that it glittered like a faery castle, and on seeing this I forgot the cold and mud and fair flew down the hill, arriving at the gates of the palace to find a procession of carriages, coaches and litters all waiting to enter. Indeed, there were so many conveyances waiting in line that lots of their passengers had disembarked and were going through the palace gates on foot, which this was fortunate for me, as I was able to join them and have it appear that I, too, had just stepped out of a carriage.

Once through the gates I tucked back my cloak so that my gown could be seen the better and entered the vast courtyard, breathless with excitement. My first feeling was of relief that I'd been given something to wear by my new friend, for even the best of my every-day gowns would have seemed very dowdy compared to what was being worn there. Men and women alike glowed with colour, their garments heavily embroi-dered or bejewelled, each ruff the more extravagant, each fall of lace more frothy, each outfit seemingly more fabulous than the one it stood beside. There were people everywhere, grouped atop of the wide stone walls, on terraces, balconies and in the courtyards, gossiping, laughing, talking, and all the time surveying the far landscape for signs that the queen's party were on their way.

I stood for several moments almost overwhelmed by the crowds, then my hand was taken and I looked round to see someone dressed as Harlequin, his doublet and hose patterned all over in coloured diamonds, his face painted the same. He carried a stick with bells on the end, and waved and jingled this as he bowed and wished me good evening.

I returned this politeness with a curtsey, but was not about to be taken in so easily again. 'Who are you, Sir?' I asked.

'He whom you seek.' He put his lips to my ear and his breath, warm upon my cheek, made me quiver all over. 'Never fear. I am Tomas.'

I looked at his painted face carefully and checked the grey-silver shade of his eyes. 'Yes, I believe you are,' I said.

'There was doubt in your mind?'

'I had trouble with a duplicate of you.'

He raised blacked-in eyebrows. 'Another queen's fool?'

'Another Jack Frost.'

'And what did he want with you?'

I dropped my voice. 'He asked me about the woman I have to watch. He didn't mention her by name, but seemed to wish me to say who she was.'

'And did you . . . ?'

I shook my head vehemently. 'Of course not! I didn't say a word.'

'And was he of my height and appearance?'

I nodded. 'As much as I know of your appearance.'

He didn't pick up on this tiny rebuke. 'Then we must think further on this and be on our guard.'

'I am already!'

'Of course. And you're doing excellently well.'

We smiled at each other. 'And now we must concentrate on the evening ahead. Are you ready to enjoy yourself?' he asked.

'I am! Where shall I stand?'

He pointed above us, to the far side of the courtyard. 'A fair number of the queen's ladies are on that terrace, so I suggest that you go there to get the best view of Her Grace's arrival.'

'She will enter through these castle gates?'

He nodded. 'So the Lord Chamberlain says. She'll then go under the stone arch and be escorted on to the platform, where she'll watch some entertainment before going upstairs to join her ladies for supper.'

I tried to make my enquiry sound casual, so that anyone who overheard us would not know the import of it. 'And what of that certain lady?'

'She is wearing emerald green velvet, with a spray of feathers on her fair hair.'

I glanced across to the terrace that he'd indicated, but there was a press of people there and I couldn't see anyone in that shade of gown. 'Is she truly there?' I asked.

'She is. *Now* she is. But in an hour's time she may not be, so when you discover her, watch her closely.' He stood back a little and took in my appearance. 'You are looking very fine, Lucy, and will find yourself in equally elegant company. Come, I'll escort you to the steps.' And so saying, he took my arm and led me through the throng towards a stone staircase twisting its way up to the terrace.

Pausing at the foot of it I suddenly became afeared. 'Supposing I am noticed and suspected?'

He shook his head. 'There are hundreds of people here tonight: some who live and work in the palace, many more invited guests and some who've come along just to glimpse the queen. A lone girl will not stand out in such a pell-mell.' He smiled. 'Even though she might be a very pretty one.'

I felt my cheeks colour. 'And . . . and will I see you again tonight to tell you what occurred?'

'Undoubtedly,' he said before he disappeared back into the crowds.

I climbed the stone staircase, which was very steep, with as much elegance as I could muster. At the top I found myself on a paved terrace alongside perhaps forty or fifty other people all excitedly awaiting Her Grace's arrival, and I leaned on the parapet here and tried to make myself as unobtrusive as possible.

After a moment, the lady I was standing beside touched my arm. It was certain that she was not my quarry, for this lady was above middle age and wore a deep red dress enlivened by embroidered Tudor roses. "Tis most exciting, is it not?' she said. 'And there are fireworks later, I've heard.'

'I have never seen fireworks!'

'But have you seen Her Grace before?' Before I could reply to this she went on, 'I have never seen her in my life, and would not be here now but my daughter is newly made a dressmaker at the palace, and it was she who bid me come along tonight.'

'Your daughter helps make the queen's gowns?'

The woman nodded proudly. 'Although there are many seamstresses in the sewing room. Eight women alone to stitch the royal buttonholes!'

We stood admiring the scene below us, pointing and exclaiming by turn. Several musicians were grouped together on a farm cart, tuning their instruments, and on another was set some scenery and furniture so that it looked like a room in a grand house. Indeed, I was so fascinated by what was going on below that for several moments I forgot what I was there for, then, suddenly remembering, turned to study the young ladies who were standing on the terrace. I saw green gowns – but not velvet. And velvet gowns aplenty – but not green. And then a little huddle of people parted and I saw a girl standing apart from anyone else, also looking down into the courtyard. She was tall, slender and dressed in a gown of bright emerald velvet with a jewelled belt at her waist and a high, flyaway ruff. Her hair, pale blonde, was set up with feathers. As if to confirm I was looking at the right girl, someone called from the group, 'Madeleine! Look here!' and she turned and smiled at the speaker. She had a lovely face – but was somewhat troubled in her mind, I thought, although I had no idea how the latter notion came to me.

I moved my head slightly, as if looking elsewhere, but concentrating all my attention on her. *This* was Mistress Madeleine Pryor; the girl I had to follow. Where would she lead me? Was she – though seemingly lovely and innocent – an enemy to our queen? Was she part of a larger plan to put Mary Queen of Scots on the throne of England?

It didn't seem possible. But how could I tell?

A heavy cart came through the gates and trundled over the cobbles, coming to rest just before the platform on which the queen was to stand. On this cart was a great barrel of earth and, growing out of this, a full-sized evergreen tree, tall as a house, pinned here and there with paper blossoms.

'Why ever is that tree there?' my companion in red asked as they removed the dray horses that had pulled the cart.

I shook my head, then said in surprise. 'I believe I see someone sitting in it!'

From behind us came some laughter, and I turned to see a stout, elderly man wearing a black velvet doublet glossed with silver embroidery. 'That is poor Lord Stamford,' he said to us. 'Two years ago the queen was so greatly displeased with him that she banished him from Court, and now he seeks to regain his place in her heart.'

'By sitting in a tree?' I asked.

'Not only that. I believe he is to perform a pretty song commending Her Grace's charms, and also recite a poem seeking her forgiveness.' He sighed. 'Ah, 'tis a terrible thing to be banned from Court!'

'Indeed!' the older woman said. 'My daughter told me that only this week Her Grace had shut someone in the Tower for daring to marry without her consent.'

'Aye,' said the portly man. 'That's young Elsbeth George. She is in the Tower, and her husband is fled to France to escape the queen's wrath!'

'But what was their crime?' I asked.

'Just to marry, I believe,' said the woman.

The man looked down at his velvet doublet and

brushed it with a fussy, finicky motion. 'If I may attempt to explain. It appears that our Gloriana – may God bless her name – does not wish to marry at the moment. While she keeps her single status, she holds her virginity very dear and expects her ladies to do the same.' He lowered his voice. 'She also expects unstinting love and attention from the men who surround her. If one of them marries, then that means one less suitor for herself.'

'They cannot all be her suitors!' I said.

He laughed. 'Do you not think so? But we all adore her! You should see us clustering around her like drones around a bumble bee.' He sighed again. 'The Court is like the sun – 'tis the centre of all glory.'

'So they say,' the woman returned.

'And are you, too, Sir, one who craves the queen's love?' I asked.

He shook his head. 'Alas, I am too old! And when I was not, I was not sufficiently well-born, nor rich, nor elegant enough to attract the queen's attention.'

'You need all those attributes, then?' I asked, somewhat amused.

'All those and more. Her Grace likes a man to be handsome, and beyond that he must also be a wit, poet, musician, dancer, linguist, horseman and tennis player. Ah, and he should have Italian manners.'

''Tis difficult to be *all* those things!' the woman and I exclaimed almost as one.

''Tis damned difficult! And 'tis only the Master of

151

the Queen's Horse, Robert Dudley, who has managed to stay the course over these past years. He remains the most loved and favoured courtier of them all.'

'But my daughter said there are rumours about Dudley . . .' the woman murmured, and the man alighted on this eagerly.

'Indeed! There are rumours everywhere that he has secretly married, and if that is true and Her Grace discovers it . . . well, there will be greater fireworks about the palace than ever you will see tonight.'

I looked at him, marvelling, anticipating conveying all this gossip to Isabelle. Was the queen's French suitor not enough, then? Did she wish to retain Robert Dudley as her lover as well? And what of he? If he had married, was it for love, or just to get even with the queen?

'You say Her Grace will not marry,' I said, 'but what about the French suitor who has come a-wooing with a bag of pearls?'

'There you have said it: *French*,' said the man. 'French and Catholic. Though Her Grace seems fond of him and will take his pearls, I wager she will not marry him in the end.'

'She is coming!' someone in the crowd shouted. A ragged cheering broke out from the balconies and terraces and, looking to the horizon, I saw bobbing lights in the distance which, coming closer, turned out to be a small party on horseback riding across the park with lanterns aloft.

The tension and excitement grew and, as the riders neared the palace, bells from the nearby churches began ringing and the musicians below us struck up a tune. Hearing this, everyone within the courtyard set up a frenzied cheering which, had we been inside, would surely have lifted the very rafters.

Her Royal Majesty the Queen of England was within our sights!

Chapter Twelve

I joined in the excited cheering and waving, all the while watching Mistress Pryor to see if there was less fervour in her greeting; to see, perhaps, if her heart was elsewhere and she responded to the arrival of Her Grace with less enthusiasm than did everyone else. I could not detect a whit of difference, however.

The little group on horseback paused at the gateway and was greeted by a tall man wearing the queen's livery, who our male companion said was the Lord Chancellor. Bowing very low, he unrolled and read out a parchment commending Her Grace's return to Richmond and acknowledging that, of all her palaces, it was her favourite. In flowery language it bade Her Royal Majesty the compliments of the season and announced that the festivities which followed were the first of twelve nights of revelry to be enjoyed before the Court moved to Whitehall in January.

This speech over, the men surrounding the queen slipped from their horses, but she stayed on her white mount and was led by a man dressed in black and gold ('Robert Dudley!' everyone whispered) towards the platform in the centre of the courtyard. I stared very hard at him, hoping to see something of the charm and charisma which made him the favourite of the queen, but could not, for although he held himself proudly and was dressed mighty fine, with shining buttons on his doublet and glittering braiding across his chest, he was too old and grey for me to consider handsome.

The queen, in black and ermine riding jacket, was helped from her horse and escorted to a throne which had been set upon the platform. As she sat down, we all – inside the courtyard and without, wherever we were standing – set up a cheering and a cry of 'God bless Your Majesty!' which was given so fervently and lovingly that it brought a tear to my eye.

Her Grace looked round at us and silence fell. 'I thank you all, my good and faithful people,' she said, then added, 'You may well have a greater prince, but you shall never have one who loves you more than I do.'

We were all much affected by these words, and I saw several lusty men reduced to tears. Under the cover of feeling in my pocket for a kerchief, I stole a glance at Mistress Pryor and saw that she, too, was dabbing at her eyes. So either she loved Her Grace as entirely as everyone else – or was feigning very well indeed.

There was a little pause while a fur-lined purple

cloak was placed around Her Grace's shoulders by a maid of honour, following which she was joined on the stage by those gentlemen who had escorted her. All were of noble stature, great striding men who seemed very well aware of their own worth in the world. The portly man behind us named them Hatton, Essex and Ralegh, though I could not have said which one was which.

As all the courtyard grew hushed, I was charmed to see Tomas appear in front of the stage with about twenty little children dressed in white. He set them in their proper places with some difficulty, for they kept wandering off, sitting down or engaging each other in conversation, thus eliciting much amusement from the crowd. Once settled, however, they sang a carol, and then a Christmas greeting to Her Grace, their pure voices floating upwards and enchanting us all. The songs over, they were invited on to the stage and allowed, each in turn, to kiss the queen's hand. Most did so, although two or three were just too young and overawed to do such a thing and ran away before they could be called forward.

There was more laughter at this and I glanced to Mistress Pryor. Yes, she was still there, leaning on the balustrade, applauding and laughing along with everyone else.

Tomas disappeared with the last of the children and, the musicians striking up anew, about eight lads and lasses came on dressed in country style as milkmaids and shepherds and carrying Christmas garlands and coloured ribbands. They proceeded to dance a pretty set before the queen, criss-crossing the ribbands they held and dancing to and fro with much agility. Sometimes the fellows lifted the girls so high that a flurry of white petticoats, stockings and coloured garters could be seen, which set all the men in the audience a-cheering.

I turned again to look for Mistress Pryor and saw her still applauding. When would she leave? Would she go at all? She must, I thought, be a very brave woman if she would secretly plot against Her Grace in the midst of her own Court. But then, if she held Mary Queen of Scots to be the true queen she would probably do anything to see her on the throne – in the same way that I, too, would be prepared to lay down my life in *my* queen's interests.

A woman clothed all in white and silver, wearing a headdress of snowy-white flowers, came on the stage next and announced that she represented the Spirit of Winter. She handed Elizabeth a key, said it was the key to the hearts of all her people, and sang a beautiful song, but this was all in a foreign language and I did not understand what it was about. Her Grace evidently did, however, for she applauded very much at the end and spoke to the woman for several minutes.

Next came a wonderful amount of birdsong, which caused the men on the stage to stare at the skies and cup their hands to their ears theatrically, as if they were filled with wonder at such a sublime noise. It was not clear where it was coming from, for none of the musicians seemed to be playing, and I asked my lady friend if she thought it was a nightingale, and if so, how she thought it could sing on cue.

'It is not a bird. It is Stamford! It is Stamford singing his heart out!' whispered the man with us, and as the birdsong continued, the leaves on the false tree shook and shivered. When it stopped, the branches parted and a man was revealed sitting on a branch. He was dressed as a minstrel in red silk doublet and hose, and carried a lute.

'Your Grace, I seek your pardon,' he called, sounding very humble, and read a sonnet asking for forgiveness. After this, playing a plaintive tune upon his lute, he sang a song which complimented the queen on her wit, her elegance and her beauty, ending with the plea that he might return to her side and be one of her favoured circle once more.

As the last notes of this died away, all eyes were on the queen to see what her reaction might be, and there were several moments of silence during which Her Grace seemed to be considering her answer. At last, however, she smiled, rose to her feet and went over to the tree, where she offered the singer her hand so that he might climb down.

Everyone cheered mightily at this, for although not many would have heard of the man nor know why he'd been banished, the exceedingly cheerful mood of the evening meant that had England's great enemy the King of Spain come by then, he, too, would probably have been forgiven for his sins. Yes, and given a bag of treasure, as well.

Stamford knelt before the queen, then seized her hand and kissed it effusively before she bade him rise and join the other men on the platform.

I looked back to my quarry, standing at the balustrade. Was she really conspiring against Her Grace? How was that possible? Such was my devotion that I couldn't envisage a world where the queen wasn't loved and admired more than any other living person.

I returned my attention to the platform, wondering what was coming next. It was a chill night but the proximity of so many others and the sheer excitement of what was going on were enough to warm me through. A play followed: a story enacted on the other cart which purported to show members of a family sitting around a dining table having their supper. There was much discord between them, many arguments and oaths, with the father of the family bitterly complaining to his wife and children of this and that. Suddenly, however, an angel appeared from a trapdoor in the cart and counselled them all to love each other, and following this they vowed to make friends and live in unity ever after. This was acted in a seemly manner and easy to understand, but I could not accept the sentiments therein, for I knew that my father would never suddenly become mannerly, kind or generous, whether appealed to by one angel or ten.

The play finished and, as the cart was rolled away, there was a sudden noise like a gunshot – nay, a score of gunshots together – making us gasp or cry out. The only one who didn't seem disturbed was Her Grace – but, of course, she had seen fireworks before.

A puff of smoke went up from somewhere to the right of the platform, then a sheet of pink flame, and everyone murmured in admiration and made themselves ready so that the next great commotion would not catch them unawares. This came as a comet trailing orange and yellow sparks, and after this a wheel of fire, then a vast column of coloured sparks accompanied by a tremendous rush of noise. There was great applause and cheering at these violent and fiery explosions (which went some way to drown the screaming of frightened children) in spite of the fact that they sent sparks in every direction and one lady's gown began smouldering.

The display lasted several minutes, only stopping when another great comet-like object hurtled sideways instead of upwards and, falling on to a thatched pig-barn on the other side of the wall, set it alight. All the pigs could be heard running out, squealing and grunting, and in a moment the roof was blazing high and bright. There was great alarm, of course, in case the fire spread towards the palace, and people immediately began running for buckets and organising themselves into a chain to bring water from the river to put it out.

It was then, in the midst of all this chaos and while the queen was being escorted safely inside on the arm of Robert Dudley, that I turned and realised that Mistress Pryor had disappeared.

I stared at the space where she'd been, furious with myself, muttering a curse under my breath at my own stupidity and making my female companion look at me in surprise.

I murmured an apology, ran down the steps and pushed through the throng, searching for a woman in a green velvet gown. She was not there, however; she had fled, and I was deeply embarrassed and ashamed. I'd failed Tomas and, to my mind, failed Her Grace also.

'I was watching her all the time,' I said to Tomas, very contrite. 'I hardly took my eyes off her but for a minute.'

Tomas shrugged. He was disappointed, I could tell, but was trying to make light of it. 'Mistress Pryor is very good at disappearing. She's already escaped from me twice.'

'I'm so sorry, Tomas.'

'You're forgiven,' he said. 'You're new to this game.'

'I promise I won't fail the next time. There will *be* a next time?' I asked anxiously.

'Of course. You are coming to the palace with Dr Dee and his partner, are you not?'

I nodded.

'Perhaps you'll have occasion to follow Mistress

Pryor then. But now you must go home, for the fire's been put out and the courtyard is emptying fast. He felt in his pocket and pulled out a silver coin, which he gave to me. 'Use part of this to hire someone to light you home, and keep the rest in case you need it on another occasion.' Hailing a passing lackey, he asked him to find a link-boy to see me safely back to Mortlake, and I thanked him very much, though I *had* been hoping that he'd have taken me home himself. Instead, however, I was wished goodnight in a kind enough way, but with no kiss, nor even clasping of hands.

I'd hoped that Mistress Midge would have retired for the night, for, my mind full of the sights that I'd seen, I wanted to go straight to bed and think of them all. I did not, besides, want to have to make up any tales of how Isabelle and I had gone a-mumming around the streets. In spite of the late hour, however, Mistress Midge was still in the kitchen, sitting on her usual stool before the kitchen fire and looking very glum.

'Are you still here?' I said, pulling my cloak tight around me so that she wouldn't see my fine gown. 'I thought you'd be abed long ago.'

She sighed. 'I'm fair mouldered with tiredness,' she said, 'but the news has made me so out of sorts that I know I won't sleep.'

I looked at her in alarm. 'What is it? Has something happened to one of the girls?'

'Oh no,' she said. 'Nothing like that. 'Tis just that

the Walsinghams aren't coming to dinner after all.'

'Not coming!' I cried, thinking of the amount of food we'd prepared and set on shelves in the cold room, the pickled oysters, the peacock, the roasted calf's head, the sugared flowers, coloured jellies and sweetmeats – not to mention the greenery around the house, the new table linen and glassware and the *venison*. 'Why ever not?'

'Sir Francis must remain with Her Grace, for she has ordered that all her gentlemen are to stay at the palace until Twelfth Night.'

'Oh,' I breathed, and though I was sorry that I wouldn't be seeing the mighty Sir Francis Walsingham, I was also somewhat relieved, for I knew the day would have been full and very fraught.

'Dr Dee is very much vexed, for he'd set his heart on having a noble family come to eat the queen's meat,' said Mistress Midge despondently.

'But . . . well, we've been saying all along, haven't we, that 'tis far too much work for us and that we'd never manage it all?'

She nodded grudgingly. 'We have.'

'Then isn't this good news?'

'But to let us know *now*, at this hour, when we have enough foodstuffs in the cold room to feed King Harry's Army. The waste of it all!'

'So who will be at the table for dinner?' I asked.

She spat into the fire. 'That dog-in-a-doublet Kelly – but he hardly counts, because he's always here – Mr

Sylvester, Mistress Allen – the toad-faced strumpet – and the master, mistress and children.'

'That's seven in all.'

'Seven. And it should have been near double that, with the Walsinghams.'

'Then we've got away lightly. And there will be plenty of food left over for us!'

Hearing this, Mistress Midge cheered up somewhat. And I went to my bed and hardly slept, my mind full of fireworks and excitement.

Chapter Thirteen

Christmas day dawned and passed much like any other, for servants do not keep Christmas. To them it merely means two church services to be fitted into their day instead of one, and more cooking, cleaning, fire-making and fetching of water if their family have visitors staying.

Waking up on Christmas morn at the bellman's five o'clock call, I immediately thought of Ma and wondered what she would be doing, for this was my first Christmas away from home. The day would not be much different for her, either, for although she didn't work as a servant, she cut and stitched a pair of gloves every day of her life, come winter or summer, snow or sun. The only difference to her mornings came if my father had been shut in the lock-up the previous night for being drunk, was in the stocks being pelted with rotten fruit, or lying half-senseless in a ditch, waiting for someone to find him. These memories made me very melancholy about my ma's life, so I said a quick prayer for her safety and rose to begin that day's chores.

Late that afternoon I was called into the library to be told how I was to assist Dr Dee and Mr Kelly at the palace. My master, I knew, was not easy in his mind about carrying out such a deception, but as I entered, Mr Kelly was busy assuring him that it would serve to bring their powers to the attention of a greater following of clients. 'And 'tis only anticipating our own transmuting of gold – for we will surely be able to do this for ourselves very soon.'

'*Will* it be soon?' Dr Dee asked wearily.

'Aye, it will, Dee. Just as soon as you've interpreted correctly all that the angels have told us.'

I was standing before them during this exchange, waiting for my instructions, and saw Dr Dee frown and sigh at this comment. He looked up at me with rheumy eyes. 'I am proud to inform you,' he said ponderously, 'that I, together with Mr Kelly, am to attend on Her Majesty at Richmond Palace on New Year's Eve.'

I didn't reply, just looked suitably awe-struck.

'We have decided that you should accompany us.'

I gave a little gasp of excitement at this, which I did not have to fake, for I'd heard nothing since that day in the library, and had been wondering if the trip to the palace would really happen.

'At the palace there will be a service you can perform for us.'

'Certainly, Sir,' I said, bobbing a curtsey.

Mr Kelly stepped forward and looked at me critically. 'You have . . . some more appropriate dress?'

By this I supposed that he meant something other than my drab workaday gown.

'I have, Sir,' I replied, for I had already decided to wear Miss Charity's green velvet.

He looked at me doubtfully, perhaps thinking that I was going to show them up. 'Servants always look their best in their master's livery,' he muttered to Dr Dee. 'And, at least, all dressed the same, there is no doubt who they belong to.'

'There are not normally enough servants in this house for the supplying of liveries,' came the reply.

'Now. Where are the rings I purchased?' Mr Kelly muttered, and I tried to curb my impatience – for I had twenty jobs waiting in the kitchen – while he felt through each of his doublet pockets and eventually put two rings: a coarse, cheap metal one and a fine gold one on to the table. 'This is just a little . . . er . . . game we are playing with the Court,' he said to me. 'A game whereby a metal ring will be substituted for a gold one.'

'I see, Sir.'

'You should manage it easily enough, for 'tis quite a simple task.'

I nodded. Simple, I thought, but risky. For what if I got caught out in some dishonest dealing in front of Her Grace?

'Tell the girl how things will proceed, Kelly,' Dr Dee

said. He glanced down at some chart he was working on. 'The whole business is your affair.'

'And when it proves a success it will become yours, I suppose?' Mr Kelly retorted.

A sniff came as answer to this. Mr Kelly turned back to me and said, 'Dr Dee and I will set up our alembic on a table before the Court, and I will explain to them some of the complex calculations involved in the changing of metal to gold.'

'You must say that it cannot always be performed,' said Dr Dee gruffly, 'or we will find ourselves being required to change pewter and copper plates into gold ones, and then where will we be?'

'Of course we will explain that, at this time, only small objects are able to be changed,' Mr Kelly replied with some scorn.

'And likewise say that all our calculations and reckonings have been done beforehand, so that they may begin to appreciate the complex issues involved.'

'Yes, yes. That as well, Dee,' said the other impatiently, and the two of them glared at each other for some moments.

'Following this, holding aloft the dark mirror, we'll call upon certain spirits to come through and change the base metal for the precious.'

I asked, 'And what do you want me to do, Sir?'

'I am just coming to that,' said Mr Kelly. 'This metal ring,' he pointed, 'will be held in a glass dish in the centre of a connected group of glass beakers. Steam will be generated from one of these which will hide the ring from view. Do you understand so far?'

I nodded briefly, thinking that the children's monkey would have understood thus far.

'While Dr Dee and I explain to the Court what we're doing, you will collect the equipment we've been demonstrating with and, as you do so, you must slip your hand in the bowl and substitute this metal ring . . .' he held it aloft, '. . . for the gold one.'

I nodded again.

'Is that quite clear?'

'Perfectly clear, Sir.'

'Then try it out, girl. Try it out,' said Mr Kelly. 'See if you can do it.'

I did as he asked, putting the gold ring on my little finger, slipping my hand into the bowl, picking up the metal one with my index finger and leaving the other behind. They made me go over these movements many times, just as they had done when I was to be the wraith of Miss Vaizey, until they were satisfied, and only then did Dr Dee say I could go back to my duties.

As I went out I heard Mr Kelly say, 'We must make sure that she practises every day, for one is never sure how much can be retained in a mind which is taken up with – bah! – nothing but ribbands and gee-gaws."

The following morning Mistress Midge and I were set to rise early to begin preparations for the grand dinner, and, waking at four o'clock, I thought to get ahead with my chores by getting up and dressed at this time. Much to my surprise, however, our cook was ahead of me and had already lit the big fire in the kitchen in readiness for the venison to be roasted. A new spit had been purchased for this and Margaret, Isabelle's little sister, was coming in to turn and baste the beast. It was more usual, of course, to have a dog to do this work, and one had been found running about the riverbank the week before and enticed inside with scraps in order to be trained. Once in the kitchen, however, Tom-fool had leapt on to its back and clung there like a jockey on a racehorse, causing the poor dog to run away yelping with fright and never be seen again.

The fire now burning well, Mistress Midge went out to the side passageway of the house, calling for me to come and help her carry the venison into the kitchen. I dusted my hands in flour and was on my way to join her when I heard a sudden anguished cry of 'No! Oh, my Lord above!'

I flung open the door, fearing that the errant dog had run off with our royal meat, but the great carcass was still hanging there on its hook. 'Whatever's wrong?'

'The venison. Lord above! 'Tis tainted!'

I sniffed deeply at the carcass then drew back in horror, for it smelled very ill – like the bodies of dead dogs which have been left overlong on the streets in a hot summer.

Mistress Midge staggered backwards, her usually ruddy face pale. 'I'm a dead woman!' she cried. 'I'll be blamed for this for sure . . . charged with letting the royal venison go bad.'

'But how did it happen?' I asked. ''Twas only delivered here a week or so back – and it has not been in the heat.'

'But when did Her Grace catch her deer? For all you and I know it has been hanging in the royal store since summer.' She gave a low, moaning sound. 'I am lost. Finished! Dr Dee speaks of nothing but this beast, and everything in the meal is to complement it. I will lose my job for sure.'

I stared first at her, then the carcass, with horror. 'Is there anything that might overcome the taste?' I asked. 'How would it be if it were cooked, sliced and a strong sauce poured over?'

'They would detect it! And besides, 'twould still be tainted underneath. With Mistress Dee's weak stomach it might poison her.' She groaned. 'I should have noticed it before, but with everything else there was to do I did not. I've worked my fingers down to their very bones and have been fair light-headed with work these past days . . .'

On and on she went, until Margaret and Isabelle arrived, for no one had thought to inform them that, there being only seven for dinner, their services were no longer needed. I was happy to see her, for I had much to tell my friend about my trip to the palace – but those stories would have to wait until we could speak in secret, of course.

The sorry tale of the venison was recounted by Mistress Midge, with much sighing and lamenting. 'My master will be up soon and will have to be informed of what's happened,' she finished. 'And when he hears, then that'll be the end for me.'

'But there is so much else to eat,' Isabelle said, looking around her at the menagerie of foodstuffs covering every available work surface. 'And you say there will only be seven at table?'

'Aye. But Dr Dee has anticipated eating that venison more than any other food, for it was given him by the queen and is almost holy in his eyes.'

'He'll say that we haven't cared for it properly,' I added.

Isabelle frowned momentarily, then her face cleared. 'Of course! The venison being tainted, we must make new!'

Mistress Midge snorted.

'Only listen,' Isabelle went on eagerly. 'Sometimes they serve roast venison at the tavern where I wash the pots, and they charge double for it over ordinary meat – for everyone knows 'tis the queen's beast, and rare.'

The cook and I both nodded.

'But 'tis not real venison, but only mutton, boiled and coloured.'

'Never!'

''Tis so.' She looked round at us, excited. 'And I know how they do it, for the tavern-keeper's wife showed me how. Do you have a side of mutton in your cold store?'

Mistress Midge nodded. 'I was serving shoulder of mutton with oysters as a side dish.'

'Well, you must take the piece of mutton, steep it in small-beer and vinegar, then parboil it in a pan with some violet colouring. When 'tis roasted over the fire and cooked through, no one will know the difference. No, not even if Her Royal Majesty herself was to dine on it!'

'Glory!' Mistress Midge said, planting several hearty kisses upon Isabelle. 'We are saved!'

The tainted venison was carried out to the river and thrown in before it was fully light, then the false venison prepared and cooked under Isabelle's direction (although it proved difficult, but not impossible, to keep Dr Dee out of the kitchen). At noon – following much anguish, swearing, blaspheming and roaring – all was ready and the table in the dining room groaned under a dish containing a calf's head, a soused heron, a bowl of oysters, two pigeon pies, a dish of larks, a varied selection of sweet and almond tarts and fancies, and the gilded marchpane cake. At the top of the table, in front of where Dr Dee would sit, a silver platter contained slice upon slice of 'roast venison', its succulent meat – dark, with a hint of purple – seeming to symbolise its royal origin, and all covered with Mistress Midge's special, royal, galandine sauce.

'It is,' said that lady, surveying it from the doorway, 'a table to be proud of. A table as might be seen in any of the grandest houses in Europe.'

It was apparent that the diners thought so too, for after the meal Mistress Midge was called into the dining room and presented with the compliments of everyone there, Dr Dee speaking lyrically of the succulence and vast superiority of the venison over any other meat in the world and saying that the fact that the animal had been killed by the queen's own fair hand gave it a special flavour all of its own, which everyone had remarked on.

The meal being completed, we washed the dishes and then set ourselves the task of eating all that had been left. This was some considerable amount, for the two pies had not even been cut into. Mistress Midge then fell asleep in front of the kitchen fire and Margaret took the monkey for a walk outside, leaving me and Isabelle to gossip (with much talk of Robert Dudley's suspected marriage) until late.

Mr Sylvester had been invited into the library to speak and share his learning with Dr Dee and Mr Kelly and wasn't seen again until past six o'clock, when, before leaving, he came to pay his respects to Mistress Midge and thank her once again for the meal – which behaviour we thought most courteous and gentlemanly. To confirm our opinion, he also left a silver sixpence for those who'd laboured in the kitchen and, seeing him to the front door and handing him his high hat and cape lined in red silk, I thanked him for this.

'Not at all!' he said in most cheerful fashion, swaying slightly, for he'd probably drunk a little too much Rhenish. 'I dined like a royal today!'

'Indeed, Sir,' I nodded. 'But at Court I expect they eat on gold and silver plates, and have drinking glasses made of crystal.'

'Court!' he said, seizing on that word. 'Spare me tales of Court, do, for there everything is pretence and artifice, and people only speak to lie.'

'I can't think you really mean that, Sir,' I said.

'Oh, but I do! At Court, all is false – and even love is decried and despised. I hate that foul world and will never enter it again!'

I was taken aback at the bitterness in his tone, when previously he'd been so merry, and wondered to myself again if, hating the Court so much, he also hated the queen . . .

Chapter Fourteen

It was near eleven in the morning on New Year's Eve that I rode with Dr Dee and Mr Kelly to the palace in an uncovered carriage, they not disguising the fact that they scorned being seen travelling with a servant. I rode alongside the driver, sitting beside the boxes which contained their equipment, and heard Dr Dee and Mr Kelly quarrelling and bickering all the way there, as bad as any married couple.

Alighting, and having two servants taking the boxes, we were ushered through the courtyard I'd been in a few nights previously, then taken along corridors and through rooms, seeing innumerable servants and many other persons who were so well-dressed they must have been invited guests. Some were masked and dressed in strange attire, some disguised as animals; there was also a family of dwarves, a troupe of acting men, some morris dancers in gay costume and a woman with a small, docile bear on a lead. Mr Kelly paused now and then to stare after one or other of them, professing himself mortified at the company he found himself in. 'Mere entertainers and travelling players,' he said. 'Gypsies and fire-eaters, quack doctors, card sharps and strumpets. What have I been reduced to?'

'You have long spoken of your wish to be invited to the palace, Kelly,' Dr Dee reminded him.

'But this is no better than being a player at a travelling show, or a base varlet who cries mousetraps in the street!' he exclaimed.

We were eventually shown into a huge room I heard called a throne room, which was high and wide as a church. People were grouped together here, coming and going from each other with much in the way of flourishing, bowing and curtseying. I was not at all sure of the day's sequence of events or when I might be called upon to assist in our demonstration of the changing of metal into gold, but, on Dr Dee and Mr Kelly finding themselves some notable gentlemen to speak to, I moved away and made myself as unobtrusive as possible in the background, while watching at every moment for both Tomas and Mistress Pryor.

There was much to see. At one end of the room was a raised dais, and on this a group of musicians were playing a merry air. At the other end was a larger platform, on which stood a gilded throne, and hanging above this a magnificent canopy of purple silk, ruched and splendidly embroidered, bearing a representation of the queen's crown of state. On the platform also was a table covered with the queen's New Year gifts – oh, so many gifts that I could not stop my jaw from dropping at the sight of them. There were objects of all shapes and sizes, wrapped and unwrapped, large and small, and amongst them I saw silver and pewter plate, clocks, jewelled boxes, crystal vases and musical instruments. I could have stayed looking for much longer, but mindful of my ma's oft-repeated observation that it was rude to stare, at last forced myself to turn away from these delights.

On a window seat sat a group of immaculate, bejewelled ladies-in-waiting, sitting as close to each other as their farthingales would allow and seeming to be sharing confidences. I watched them, admiring them greatly and sighing a little inside because of it, for I knew that no matter how fine a gown I wore, my nails would still be torn, my hands chapped, my speech inelegant and my skills in the feminine arts non-existent. I could never be like them, I thought, remembering Tomas's words when he'd explained that it would be impossible for someone of my background to become a lady-in-waiting. And so surely it was also impossible, came the thought, that Tomas should mean anything with his sweet talk and his hand-kissing, for wasn't that part of his role: to flatter and to pay little compliments in order to bring a smile to a lady's lips – even when, like me, she clearly wasn't a lady?

Shortly after I'd reasoned this, Tomas entered the

room with a tiny woman, no bigger than a child of six, on his arm. He was masked and again wearing the Harlequin outfit, and the little woman was partnered with him as Columbine and dressed in a satin gown of quite startling yellow, with everything about her in miniature, from the tip of her jewelled headpiece down to her feet in minute satin shoes. I'd never seen such a delightful and engaging creature in all my life before, not even at a fair, and could not stop from staring whilst she and Tomas promenaded around the floor, drawing all eyes to them.

There was much clapping from the floor, and calls of 'Charming!' and 'Enchanting!' before, after making two circuits of the room, Tomas led her to the platform beneath the throne. She sat down on the edge of this, swinging her legs, and hadn't been there more than a moment before she was approached by one of the queen's ladies-in-waiting who, lifting her as if she were a doll, carried her off to a window alcove.

''Tis the queen's dwarf, Tomasina,' said a woman standing nearby, noticing my fascination. 'Have you not seen her before?'

I shook my head.

'Her Grace is most fond of her. She has a bed in Her Grace's apartment and is always taken on progresses.'

I curtseyed to my new acquaintance, who was, perhaps, in her mid-thirties and wearing a dark gown and single row of pearls. She looked neat and elegant – and 'twas therefore difficult to tell whether she was a guest or a high servant.

She asked very politely who I was, and I told her my name and that I'd come to the palace with Dr Dee.

'You work with him?' she asked, startled. 'You are some type of . . . of cunning woman?'

I shook my head quickly. 'No! I'm merely his children's nurse.'

She stood back a little and surveyed what I was wearing. 'Well, my dear, I must say that you don't dress like a nursemaid.'

I smiled. 'I have a friend who is a lady, and she gave me this gown,' I said. I hesitated, then saw no harm in telling her the truth. 'But I'm not here as a nursemaid, for I've come to help set up Dr Dee's apparatus ready for an experiment.'

'Really, my dear?'

I was torn then between curiosity and politeness, and the former won. 'And do you . . . ?' I asked, leaving the question open.

'I'm maid to one of Her Grace's maids of honour,' she said proudly.

'And have you been so for long?'

'Ten years,' was the reply. 'My young lady came to Court as a girl of twelve, and is now twenty-two.'

'Is she here now?' I asked, nodding towards the groups of ladies.

'Indeed she is,' said the woman, speaking like a proud mother. 'She is in blue velvet, with her hair coiled about her head.'

I saw the girl immediately, for although she had quite a plain face, her hair was fair and arranged most beautifully in plaits around her head, these plaits having pearls threaded through.

I gave a cry of admiration. 'Her hair is very elegant.'

'And most complicated. It took a very long time,' she confided with a sigh.

'You must have many skills and abilities.'

She nodded. 'All the lady's maids must be able to style hair, iron ruffs, mend lace and calm a high complexion. Oh, and apply a poultice to feet that have seen too much dancing,' she added with a smile.

'And is it true you're like one big family?'

She nodded and laughed. 'Mostly we are, because we love what we're doing and revere Her Grace. Sometimes, though, one or other of us is churlish and there's a falling-out – as is usual in a family.'

'Of course,' I said, and I made some other chit-chat, admiring the cut of a dress, the colour of some leather slippers, asking how the young ladies managed to keep up with fashions and so on, and all the time wondering how I could gain more knowledge of Mistress Pryor. After a short while I said, 'My cousin, who is 'prenticed to a perfumer, visited the Court once. She met a lady-in-waiting who was very kind to her, and oft speaks of it.'

'Who was that?' the woman asked.

'I believe the lady's name was Mistress Pryor. Is there anyone of that name here?'

'That would be Madeleine Pryor,' said the woman. She looked up and down the hall. 'She'll be here somewhere; I saw her earlier.' She smiled. 'You wish to give her your cousin's greetings, do you?'

'Oh no,' I said. 'I wouldn't dare to approach her! If I saw her I could tell my cousin of it, that was all.'

'Well, you'll be sure to see her, for everyone comes into the hall when Her Grace opens her gifts. Although . . .'

I glanced at her enquiringly.

'I know Mistress Pryor has been feeling rather out of sorts of late, for she oft retires early to her chamber.'

I put on an expression of concern. 'It's nothing severe, I hope.'

'I trust not, for if one young lady suffers with an ague or a fever, then they all seem to catch it. But Mistress Pryor's ailment seems to be more one of melancholy, for she is oft sad – and now that I think on it, she was so out of sorts she didn't come with us on Her Grace's progress to Kent last September.'

'My cousin will be sorry to hear that she's unwell,' I said, my mind sifting and sorting this information. Why had Mistress Pryor declined to go on the progress? Was it in order to pursue her own interests; to work secretly for the Scottish queen?

'I shall be interested to see Dr Dee,' said my new companion. 'When will this amusement take place?'

I shook my head. 'I don't know whether it will be before or after the queen opens her gifts. How do these matters usually go?'

'The gifts take some considerable time, for as each is opened they are logged into a book by the Lord Chancellor.' She lowered her voice. 'By the end of it, the only one who is in the least interested in what comes out of which box is the queen herself, so the strolling players and other divertisements are to keep us from being bored while Her Grace is indulged.'

There was a sudden fanfare of trumpets and a set of double doors were flung open. Everyone turned expectantly and I held my breath, anticipating the queen and wondering what glorious gown and sumptuous jewels she'd be wearing on such an important occasion, but instead a group of five or six noblemen came through, followed by some of the queen's ladies, including, I saw with a start, Mistress Pryor. All eyes watched while they walked down the room and climbed on to the platform, the ladies dainty and elegant, the men holding themselves very high and proud.

'Her Grace will be here afore long,' said my companion in my ear. 'And there is the lady you asked for, wearing pink satin.'

I thanked her.

'And do you know who the gentlemen are?'

'Not all of them,' I replied. 'Who is the big, bear-like man with the gold chains about him?'

'That's Sir Francis Walsingham,' came the reply.

I nodded, pleased to have seen him at last. Realising then that there was someone missing, I scanned the faces once more. 'But where's Her Grace's favourite?' I asked, for Robert Dudley wasn't amongst the group on the platform.

My companion glanced quickly about her before she spoke, but no one seemed to be paying us any attention. 'He rode home to his fine castle on Christmas Day,' she said in a low voice, 'and has not been seen since.'

'I heard a rumour . . .'

She nodded, putting a finger to her lips. 'We all know of it. 'Tis no more than a rumour still, but everyone is affrighted lest Her Grace get to hear.'

'But doesn't she wonder why he isn't here at the palace?'

'He's reported to be unwell, but e'en so . . . Her Grace wants all her men in attendance over Christmastide, and has already let it be known she's most displeased with him.'

There was another fanfare of trumpets and everyone looked towards the doors once more. I picked up the front of my skirts ready to curtsey, but still the queen didn't appear. Instead, a dark-suited equerry entered, walked swiftly through the room, knelt before Sir Francis Walsingham and held out a letter.

Sir Francis bade the man rise, read the letter and spoke to him very closely and urgently for several minutes. Following this, they both conversed with the other noblemen on the platform.

By then, most of the room were watching this

scene, wondering what was happening, and though I, too, was engrossed, I made sure that I kept part of my attention on Mistress Pryor. Eventually the equerry bowed to Sir Francis and went off, followed by the other gentlemen. Sir Francis then walked to the middle of the platform and, standing with one hand on the gilded arm of the throne, appealed for silence.

When silence was achieved, he said, 'I fear Her Grace will not join us this day,' and my heart plunged for a moment, for I thought something terrible must have happened. Others must have thought it too, for there were some cries and exclamations of alarm. Sir Francis went on quickly, 'Be reassured that Her Grace has come to no harm. However, some correspondence has been discovered which, only just now decoded, has uncovered a plot whereby our royal lady would have been unseated from her throne and replaced with the usurping Queen of Scotland.'

Consternation broke out across the hall until, after a moment, Sir Francis again lifted his hands for silence. 'Rest assured that the plot was revealed before any harm could be done, and Her Grace is perfectly safe. But as she and her advisers must speak together at some length to ensure her continued safety and well-being, she will not be opening her gifts today. Nevertheless, she entreats you to stay, if you will, and enjoy the company gathered here.'

While all this speech was taking place I was watching Mistress Pryor, and as the word 'plot' was uttered, saw high colour come into her cheek. She was alarmed, I could see. Was this just because she feared the queen to be in danger – or because they had uncovered a plot that she was involved in?

As Sir Francis left the platform, disquiet filled the room. People formed and re-formed into groups, discussing the news, and I heard the word 'Catholic' uttered in anger several times. A few people left the hall by the double doors, seemingly on urgent business, and others entered. It was then that something very puzzling occurred, for I saw a figure detach himself from a group nearby, walk swiftly down the length of the room and disappear. He was a tall man wearing a short black cape lined in red silk and, though I only saw him in profile and he wore a mask, in style and bearing he seemed very much like Mr Sylvester – so much so that I could not stop myself from calling out his name. Of course, the commotion about the room was such that no one heard me, least of all him, and although my companion looked at me curiously, I merely said that I thought I'd seen someone I knew.

Could it really have been him? I wondered after. The figure had seemed very like, and certainly Mr Sylvester had a cloak the same. But . . . but only a few days past I'd heard him say that the Court was mere artifice, that he hated that foul world and would never enter it. But . . . he'd said never enter it *again*, I thought, recalling his exact words. As if he'd entered it before and found it not to his liking.

'Well,' said my companion, after we'd watched the courtiers and guests come and go about us for several moments. 'It doesn't look as if I shall see Dr Dee's demonstration after all.'

'It does not,' I said, adding that I was somewhat relieved.

'Are you going to stay longer?' she asked then, but I hardly replied to her question, so intent was I on watching Mistress Pryor. She was helped down from the platform in a gracious manner by Tomas, then made her way across the crowded room, concealed from me now and again by the groups of people between us. All was well until she reached the far wall, when she neatly – and very suddenly – disappeared behind a silk hanging. So smoothly did this move occur that if I hadn't been watching at that precise moment, I might have supposed her to have been magicked into thin air.

I paused only to say a brief farewell to my companion, then hurried across the room, slipped behind the same hanging and found myself facing an open doorway. Steps descended here and without hesitation I went down, hearing below me the tip-tapping of Mistress Pryor's shoes on the stone. At the bottom of the steps I found myself outside in a courtyard full of carts and coaches and, swiftly surveying them, saw Mistress Pryor slip into a dark-painted carriage with the driver already atop.

I gave my first thought then to Dr Dee and wondered if he'd look for me in order to go home. I decided he would not, for if he gave me any thought at all he'd surely expect me to make my own way there. Deciding this, hearing the door close behind Mistress Pryor and her voice calling to the driver to whip up the horse, I quickly climbed on to the luggage rack at the back of the carriage and made ready to hang on for as long as the journey took.

As the carriage rocked and swayed through Richmond I began to wonder if I'd done a foolish thing, and by the time the horse was stumbling through Barnes on a rutted road and I was being jolted from one side of the rack to the other, I was sure of it, for the continual movement was making me feel unwell. I was greatly relieved, therefore, when in another five minutes we came to a better road – the turnpike road to Hammersmith, I thought – and my journey became somewhat smoother.

We seemed to be somewhere in Putney when we slowed down. We were near to the river – for I could smell it in the air – and there must also have been a glue-maker's shop nearby, for I could detect the stink of boiled animal bones. Feeling the coach easing up, I braced myself to jump. I was not worried about hurting myself so much as spoiling – perhaps tearing – my beautiful gown, so I gathered as much material as possible in my arms and waited until the coach had almost stopped before I half-rolled, half-scrambled off the back and then hastily brushed myself down and smoothed out my skirts.

Dusk was falling and it was easy to conceal myself in the shadows of a doorway and from here peer out and see Mistress Pryor, most of her pale hair concealed under a hood, climb out and speak to the driver. I studied her then, and again as she walked away from the carriage, and perceived that there was something different about her manner now that she was away from the confines of the palace. Perhaps I felt this because of what Isabelle called my Sight, or perhaps I was just imagining it, but Mistress Pryor, for some reason, seemed eager, lighter in her step – and her mind, too. As if – the thought occurred to me – she was only now being her true self.

There were a few people around in the lane: boys on errands, housewives late with their shopping, a peddler selling ribbands, and as Mistress Pryor moved off I sauntered amongst these, pretending interest in a near-by shop window. She turned into a long passageway which sloped up and away from the river and appeared to have several alleyways going off it, and I followed, finding the way getting narrower and darker as it ran between tall, beamed houses, their jutting bays making them almost meet in the middle. A window opened above me and a bowl of washing water was thrown out, which splashed my gown and shoes. Stopping to shake my skirts, I saw, in the distance, Mistress Pryor go up some steps, cross a small bridge over a stream, then disappear.

It was at this point I realised that someone was

following *me*, for I heard a man's heavy footfalls behind me and the panting of someone out of breath, as if they'd been running to catch me up. Frightened, I went through a gate that was standing ajar and entered a small courtyard, hoping that whoever had been following me would presume I'd reached home, and turn away.

I concealed myself behind the gate as the heavy footfalls came closer, and the thought occurred to me that anyone involved in a plan to kill a queen would not hesitate to kill a nursemaid. I don't know why I should have thought this, for there was nothing to link my pursuer with the woman I pursued and any dire plot. Somehow, though, I felt there was a connection.

I held my breath – if I could have remembered a prayer at this time, I would have said it – and kept completely still, fearing that my pursuer might hear my heart thumping. After hesitating on the other side of the gate for some moments, however, he went on.

I tried to steady myself, for my legs were shaking and I feared they wouldn't bear my weight. I would not, I decided, come out of the courtyard until I'd counted to fifty, in case the man was still lurking nearby. I'd only got halfway through my numbers, though, when looking about me in the near-gloom I saw that a notice had been nailed to the back door of the house whose yard I sheltered in. I was immensely grateful then that I could read, or I might have halted there longer, for on this paper was marked a large red cross, and the words,

MAY GOD HAVE MERCY ON US.

Seeing this, I ran out of the courtyard as if the hounds of hell were after me, for whoever had been following me was surely not as terrifying a prospect as the plague.

'I ran off straight,' I said to Tomas later, 'and when I reached a little open square at the top of the passageway I found that Mistress Pryor – and whoever had been following me – had both disappeared. I think they may have been together . . .'

'Perhaps,' he nodded. 'There are bound to be several other people involved.'

'I'm sorry I lost her again.'

'But this time we know where she went: to somewhere close to a plague-ridden house in Putney. She won't be so difficult to find.'

'I could show you where I last saw her,' I offered.

Tomas nodded. He was not wearing the Harlequin outfit now, but was all in black, with a cloak, hat and silk hood pulled low across his face. In the darkness, he might have passed for anyone, but I knew him by his grey eyes, which reflected almost silver in the light from the candle lantern he was carrying.

'But do you think it's safe to go so near to a dwelling with plague?' I asked, realising that I'd probably found the house that Mistress Midge had told me about.

He nodded. 'Quite safe. There hasn't been a new

case for six weeks or so. And you didn't go inside the house, did you?'

'I did not! I hardly breathed at all when I was near it, and when I found Mistress Pryor had escaped me, I used some of your money for a hackney coach here.' *Here* was back at Richmond Palace, where I'd given a penny to a boy to take Tomas a message requesting that he come out and speak to me.

'All is well, then.' He smiled at me and, longing to see him more clearly, I tried to peep under his hood. He was too quick for me, however, and moved his head so that a fold of dark silk fell across his cheek.

'What of the plot that was discovered today at the palace?' I asked. 'Is Her Grace perfectly safe?'

Tomas nodded. 'She is. But the Queen of Scots has surely incriminated herself, for correspondence in her own handwriting calling for the death of the queen has been discovered between her and a gentleman named Babington. They were corresponding by means of coded messages conveyed inside a barrel of beer, and 'tis most fortunate that Walsingham's agents managed to decode them in time.'

We were silent a moment, thinking of the consequences if they had not.

'All is well, however, by the Grace of God! And now we look close to finding whatever it is that Mistress Pryor is concerned in, too.' He glanced up at the torch-lit windows of the palace. 'I must go back inside, for there is still much to talk about. Can you meet me in

Putney tomorrow and show me the last place you saw Mistress Pryor?'

I nodded eagerly.

'And the Dee family won't think it odd that you're missing?'

I shook my head. 'They won't know. They're going to Greenwich tomorrow and staying there until Twelfth Night.'

'Are you able to meet me in Putney at midday?'

'Of course.'

'Then wait near to the wharf. Try not to be too visible,' he said, and lifted my hand and kissed it.

I knew well – for I'd seen him do it often enough – that the kiss was merely a courtesy he extended to all ladies, but I was content to be one of them.

As I reached home, I remembered that I hadn't told him about the man at Court who'd looked so much like Mr Sylvester. But there was surely nothing to that . . .

Chapter Fifteen

Had the Dee family not been going away I would have been in some difficulties. I might even – in order to go to Putney and meet Tomas – have had to leave my job. Some time ago, however, the family had arranged to collect little Arthur from his wet nurse and go to stay for a few days with the children's grandmamma in Greenwich in order to celebrate the season.

That just left Mistress Midge for me to deal with, so, finding it difficult enough to sleep anyway, I rose very early and went through my work in double-quick time. This meant that by the time our cook rose, all my chores, and some of hers, were completed. She was thus in a very good mood, and I capitalised on this by asking for permission to spend the day 'with Isabelle'.

By eleven o'clock the Dee family had gone downriver in a hired wherry to Greenwich, and I was walking in their wake along the riverbank towards Putney. The day was fresh and bright and I was enjoying my walk, for there was a light breeze blowing, the sun was sparkling on the Thames and a dotting of yellow and white at the sides of the path showed where a few snowdrops and celandines had already pushed their way through the damp earth. Life had been very exciting for me lately and I was trying to reconcile myself to the fact that it might soon become rather dull, for I knew that when the queen and Court were absent from Richmond, all the life would go out of it.

In the meantime, however, what might Tomas and I discover today? Would we be instrumental in saving Her Grace from another foul plot? Thinking along these lines, my imagination was such that, there being a very quiet stretch of the river where there was no one around, I dawdled and indulged in some pretence in which I was received by the queen and thanked mightily for my brave work on her behalf.

I understand you wear my image around your neck, Her Grace would say. *Then let me reward you by replacing that tarnished silver with a medal of solid gold, which will be some small recompense for discovering this fearsome plot against me and saving my life.*

I thank you kindly, Your Grace, I'd reply, bowing low so that the medal could be slipped over my head. *But I merely did what any man or woman would do in order to preserve the life of our glorious monarch.*

And possibly . . . *One more thing. I wish to ennoble you, my child, to give you the title of Lady Lucy, and this is how you will be known for ever after.*

I then went through this scenario again, but as well as the title I received a great sum of money from the queen, enough to enable me to leave the employ of the Dee family and buy a small cottage where my ma could come to live with me in safety and happiness for the rest of her life.

Coming close to Hammersmith, there were many more people about and ferryboats plying their trade, so I ceased my play-acting. Hearing a horse coming at a gallop behind me, I stood to one side to allow it free passage, but to my surprise the horse was reined in and stopped.

'Am I on the right path for Mortlake?' the rider called to me.

I looked up. The horse was a strong grey roan, its rider a young country gentleman in tweed doublet, leather riding boots and plaid travelling cloak. His face was pleasant and he was hatless, his hair shining and dark.

'You are not, Sir,' I said, glad that he had not caught me in the midst of my fantasies. 'You are going in the wrong direction.'

I think he swore under his breath. 'Then I must turn around and go back some distance,' he said, 'for I'm bound for the house of the magician in Mortlake.'

I gave an exclamation of surprise.

'Do you know the house?' he asked. 'I believe it stands by the Thames.'

I looked up at him once more, squinting, for the sun was in my eyes and he was cast into silhouette.

'I do know it,' I said, lifting my hand to block out the sun. 'But if you wish to speak to Dr Dee, then I fear you'll find him away from home.'

'Do you say so? But wait, 'tis thoughtless of me to address you with the sun placed so in the sky.' And so saying, he swung his leg over the horse to dismount, then slid down and flexed his legs and arms a little, as if he'd been riding for some time. 'You say the good doctor is out . . . but it's not him I'm seeking.'

'Mr Kelly will not be there either.'

'Nor Mr Kelly! I am set to call on one of Dr Dee's household, a pretty maid called Lucy.'

My mouth dropped open in complete and utter surprise. 'But, Sir . . .' I began, and then I looked into this young man's face, now on a level with mine, at his mouth curved into a wide smile and his eyes, which were grey. 'Tomas!' I cried.

He burst into laughter and, after a startled and embarrassed moment, I laughed too. Then I looked at him, feeling extreme shy, for though we'd known each other for some months, this was the first time we'd come face-to-face, so to speak, with no masks, disguise or counterfeiting between us. I looked and saw that he had good features, a strong nose, broad forehead and long eyelashes – indeed, I thought, I'd be able to report to Isabelle that he was a most handsome young man.

'I could not resist it,' he said when he'd stopped laughing. 'But now I'm sorry, for you're discomforted, are you not?'

'A little,' I admitted. 'And yet 'tis not the first time you have played me so. You seem to enjoy it.'

He shrugged. 'I am a jester; the queen's fool,' he said. ''Tis my trade.'

I looked at him pensively, embarrassed at how, once again, I'd been completely taken in by him.

'I merely thought I'd bring some levity to this day!' He squeezed my hand. 'We have hard and perhaps unpleasant work ahead of us. Why shouldn't we begin it with some Tom-foolery?'

I laughed then, for what he said made sense.

He mounted the horse once more and said we'd get there quicker if I rode with him. I was offered a stirrup to climb on and a hand to pull me up and in a moment was seated before him sideways on the saddle, his hands passing around my waist and holding fast the reins.

Once there, it was impossible to be the smallest bit cross with him, for it was very pleasant clip-clopping along the river path in the winter sunshine, bidding a genial good-day to strangers and speaking together of very many things. He was open with me and did not conceal anything of his life, even telling me something of his childhood, for his father had been the late king's fool, but had died before Tomas was six years old.

On reaching Putney wharf, he tied up the horse and

gave a street urchin a coin to mind it for him, and we walked together to the few small shops where I'd begun following Mistress Pryor the day before.

'Madeleine didn't come back to the palace last night,' Tomas said as we set off along that same passageway. 'I daresay she hoped that in all the fuss over the discovery of yesterday's plot, no one would notice she was away overnight.'

'So she's still here in Putney?'

He shrugged, looking perplexed. I enjoyed watching the different expressions cross his face, for it was the first time they'd not been obscured by a mask. 'Probably,' he said. 'Unless...'

'Unless?'

'Unless yesterday's plot incriminated her in some way and as we speak she's travelling towards the Queen of Scotland.'

'Then our job would be over,' I said, rather disappointed. And I wouldn't have achieved very much at all, I thought.

I passed the place where the washing water had been thrown out, and then the gate I'd hidden behind. 'This is the courtyard,' I said, gingerly pushing open the door. 'And there's the plague notice...'

Tomas looked at it briefly. ''Tis nothing to worry about, for I made enquiries about it last night.'

'Was it true plague?'

He nodded solemnly. 'I fear it was. Three died in here, but 'twas then contained and went no further.'

Going out again, we continued between the houses until we came to the cobbled square which, that day, had stalls on it selling herbs and greenstuffs in season.

'By the time I arrived here, she was nowhere to be seen,' I said, nevertheless turning left and continuing alongside a tannery with a great amount of animal skins hanging outside.

'Then tell me, how did you know to turn left instead of right just now?' Tomas asked.

I stopped, surprised. 'I don't know. Something just told me which way to go.' As I spoke, I shook my head to clear it, remembering how, the day before, I'd some-how sensed Mistress Pryor's feelings. 'It's the strangest thing, but I almost know how she felt yesterday,' I said wonderingly. 'She was easy in her mind, because she was going towards something she loves!'

'Something she loves,' Tomas repeated, bemused. 'That doesn't sound as if she was attending a meeting of conspirators. But how is it that you know such things?'

'I just . . . feel them.' I closed my eyes for an instant. 'Mistress Pryor came along here yesterday as she's been many times before, and was hurrying, happy, for she was greatly anticipating something.'

'Something to do with Her Grace? A plot to unseat her?'

I shook my head, frowning. 'I cannot think it was that.'

We came to a crossing of lanes. 'Where now?' Tomas asked.

I closed my eyes again. Today, my instincts were stronger. Today, something within me was even more tuned to Mistress Pryor's feelings.

'This way!' I pointed assuredly. 'Past this old thatched cottage and the tumbledown stable and . . . *there*!' I said with some surprise. 'She's in there, I'm sure of it.'

We stood looking at the building I was pointing at, which was long and ancient, with ornate, arched Gothic windows.

'That was once a convent,' Tomas said. ''Twas closed some years back.'

'And where did the nuns go?'

He shrugged. 'I believe some are still allowed to live there.'

'Then perhaps Mistress Pryor merely goes to practise the old religion in secret.'

'And stays overnight?' Tomas said somewhat incredulously. 'I have known church services go on two hours or more, but not for twelve!'

'Well, she *is* there.'

'You're quite sure?'

I nodded. I did not know how I could be so certain, and yet I was convinced of it.

'Then we must catch her – and those she's with – unawares, and take them all in for questioning.' His brow furrowed. 'We don't know how many of them there are. Perhaps I should come back here later with some of the Queen's Guard.'

'But they may all have gone by then,' I said, very much wanting to do more. 'What if I got in there and tried to discover what's going on? I might at least find out who she's in league with.'

'Hmmm . . .' Tomas pondered.

'It could be our false Jack Frost!'

'But going a-spying may put you in danger.'

'Isn't that what spies are for: to listen behind doors, conceal themselves in hidey-holes and try to discover secrets?' I touched the coin at my throat. 'You know I'd dare all those things and more for Her Grace.'

Tomas frowned, his grey eyes serious. 'Suppose harm comes to you . . .'

'I shall take great care! If anyone calls me out, I'll play the simple maid – say I've come a-selling trinkets or ballads or suchlike.'

'And if they ask where these things are?'

I paused and thought for a moment. 'Very well, then. I'll say I come from the local tavern to invite those within to hot pigeon pies and gravy!'

Tomas smiled at this. 'As you wish,' he said, 'but allow me at least to assist you in gaining entry by providing some distraction,' and with no more ado he removed his tweed doublet and turned it inside out so that it showed dull of colour and with fraying seams. He then tousled his hair so that it stuck up, wind-strewn, around his head and, bending down to dabble his fingers in mud, applied some of this to one of his cheeks. In less than a moment there was an unkempt street lad standing before me, so correct in demeanour and expression that I couldn't help but burst out laughing.

Putting his finger to his lips, he bade me stand around the end of the building, so that I couldn't be seen, and knocked vigorously at the door several times. After a moment it was opened, although I could not yet see by whom.

I watched as Tomas began acting out a dumb-show to this unseen person, indicating that he had not eaten for some days and was about to expire of hunger, and going on to promise a display of acrobatics in return for something to eat. So amusing was this little show that whoever was viewing it burst into fits of girlish laughter and clapped her hands.

Tomas now stepped away from the door and into the lane, jumping over the stinking ditch that ran down its centre and indicating that he would perform under a tree there. The person who'd answered the door moved out in order to see him the better, and I saw that she was diminutive and clothed all in black, apart from a white wimple. So the building remained a Catholic stronghold, I thought to myself – and therefore an obvious meeting place for those who sought to unseat our queen and put one of the old religion on the throne . . .

Two housewives with laden baskets, seeing their was some fun to be had, halted by the tree, and Tomas began his performance by tumbling somersaults, easy and practised, seemingly as comfortable standing on his hands as on his feet. Although I would have liked to have seen all of his act, the little nun now had her back to me, so I immediately slipped through the open door of the convent and down the right-hand corridor.

As at Dr Dee's house, there was an abundance of doors, curtained stairways and hanging tapestries ahead of me (though I was not sorry to see these, knowing they'd all make good hiding places should anyone come along). Reaching halfway down this corridor I stopped for a moment and closed my eyes in order to concentrate better and listen to the sounds around me. What could I hear? Could I discern any earnest discussions, arguments or plotting? What *was* Mistress Pryor doing within these walls?

I stood for a short while and then, obeying something within me, turned and went back in the direction I'd come from, passing the front door once again and going straight on. Reaching the end of this corridor, I paused in front of a set of elaborate, glassed double doors, for something told me that Mistress Pryor would be found within.

I suppose I should have thought about my next move, planned what I'd say and do, but I was so curious about her reasons for being in this place, so anxious to find out the truth, that I didn't hesitate to push open the doors a little and peer through.

And then I gasped aloud, for within I found Mistress Pryor engaged in the most surprising act: not involved in some violent discourse on the best way to challenge Her Grace's position on the throne of England, but sitting quietly beside a window, an infant asleep in her arms!

She started up when she heard my gasp, and twisted her body away so that the child was concealed from my view. 'Who are you?' she asked, her voice high and frightened. 'What are you doing here?'

Too startled by what I'd seen, I didn't reply.

'You shouldn't be here! You must leave at once.'

I still didn't speak, or even move. On the way along the corridor I'd thought up several new reasons for being there, from bringing a message from a dressmaker to asking whether or not Mistress Pryor might wish to buy some fine quality lace. Face to face with her, however, I could not bring myself to utter any of my paltry excuses. This woman, I was now perfectly sure, held no treason in her heart. She was not an enemy of the queen, nor was she plotting to put someone else on the throne.

'I demand you answer me at once!'

'I'm sorry,' I stammered. 'I . . . I shouldn't be here at all. I have nothing to say.'

She gave a sudden cry. 'You have nothing to say! You frighten me half to death by suddenly appearing here, then tell me you have nothing to say? How did you find me? How do you come to be in this place, and what do you want?

I heaved a sigh, feeling like the worst kind of

intruder; as if I'd come to do harm to the innocent babe in her arms. 'I followed you here yesterday,' I murmured, shame-faced.

'Followed me? Why? Do you mean me harm?'

I hesitated, then felt I must tell the truth. 'It is just this. Someone suspected you of plotting against the queen, and I was asked to watch you.'

'*I* was suspected?'

I nodded.

She gave a little cry. 'But I've served the queen faithfully for seven years! I've turned down every chance of happiness to devote my life to her. And now I am suspected of being her enemy?'

The child, perhaps hearing the fear in her voice, stirred and made a small sound of distress. Immediately Mistress Pryor seemed to forget that I was there and turned to look at it, smoothing its cheek and rocking it gently in her arms.

'I am so sorry. I have no business here,' I said, backing away.

'Stop!' she said. 'You cannot leave without telling me what's behind all this. Was it Walsingham who suspected me?'

'I believe it was he – and others.'

'If they are saying that I'd harm our queen then it's *they* who are speaking treason, for I am every bit as loyal and true to Her Grace as they. More so!' And saying this, she began weeping.

I gave a low curtsey. 'Please accept my apologies. I

assure you that you will hear no more of this,' I said. I turned to go. 'And I am truly sorry I've caused you such grief.'

Her head was bent over the babe and, still weeping, she didn't reply. Deeply ashamed of the distress I'd caused her, I went to the door, only to almost collide with a gentleman coming through it. And it was then that I had my second great shock of the day when I came face to face with the children's tutor, Mr Sylvester.

Chapter Sixteen

He and I stared at each other, both utterly astonished at the other's appearance. I began to back away, feeling agitated and very much at a disadvantage. I was a mere nursemaid amongst greater folk, and in a place that I shouldn't be.

'What in Heaven's name are you doing here?' Mr Sylvester said. 'How did you find us?'

'I believe she works for Walsingham,' Mistress Pryor said, still weeping.

'What?! That can't be so. She is maid to Dr Dee's children,' said Mr Sylvester. He went over to Mistress Pryor and placed a hand on her shoulder. 'Has she upset you, sweeting?' he asked gently.

Odd and odder . . . I stared at them in some bewilderment and then I looked towards the door, wondering if I should just run away. In spite of my great unease, however, I was most intrigued at this situation, and knew that, if I ran, I might never discover answers to all the questions in my head.

'She came in here with some absurd tale of me being involved in a plot against the queen!' said Mistress Pryor.

'Never!'

''Tis so ridiculous that she may have made up the whole thing. Perhaps she is just a thief.' She looked at me searchingly, taking in my fine velvet gown. 'You say she's a nursemaid, but she's not dressed as one. She has, perhaps, stolen the clothes she wears.'

'I have not,' I protested strongly, for I greatly feared being taken and thrown into jail. 'Perhaps . . . perhaps I should explain everything to you.'

'Yes, you should,' said Mr Sylvester curtly. 'And you may begin at once.'

Ten or so minutes later, Tomas and I were sitting on a window seat facing Mistress Pryor and Mr Sylvester. I'd begun by trying to explain the situation myself, but things had gone so awkward between us that I'd asked if I might go and fetch my companion.

Both Mr Sylvester and Mistress Pryor had looked mighty startled on seeing Tomas, and he equally so on seeing Mr Sylvester. The gentlemen bowed to each other (though Mr Sylvester swore under his breath several times as he did so), and for some awkward moments after this none of us seemed inclined to speak. At last Tomas stood up and went to a light oak rocking cradle in which the babe now rested. 'How old is this small creature?' he asked.

'She is near three months old,' said Mr Sylvester.

'And named Elizabeth after our good queen, whom I love and revere,' said Mistress Pryor somewhat defiantly.

Tomas sat down beside me again, and there was another silence. 'Twas, I think, the only time I'd ever seen him at a loss for words. Eventually, he began, 'As you know, I am the queen's fool. But perhaps not so foolish when it comes to affairs of the heart.'

No one made comment on this, and he continued, 'The child, of course, belongs to you both.'

At first it seemed that Mistress Pryor might deny it, but Mr Sylvester placed his hand over hers. ''Tis too late for subterfuge,' he said, adding, 'Yes, she is our natural child.'

'And born of love!' said Mistress Pryor.

'You, Sir, I believe I recognise from Court as one Leopold Harding,' Tomas said.

Mr Sylvester nodded. 'I was dancing master at Court for nigh on a year.'

Dancing master. Then that was why, I thought, he sometimes seemed to be dressed more like a court dandy than a scholar.

'And it was then that you and Mistress Pryor . . . ?' Tomas led him gently.

He nodded. 'The truth is this: I was there to teach the ladies-in-waiting their galliards and their pavanes, and while dancing, Mistress Pryor and I fell in love.'

'And Her Grace objected?'

Mr Sylvester sighed. 'Her Grace very much objected.'

'We asked for permission to marry and she said no, and banned Leo from Court forthwith,' Mistress Pryor explained.

'Not only am I banned from Richmond, but from anywhere the Court is on progress: I am not to stay at Whitehall, Syon, Greenwich, Windsor nor Hampton Court, and if I am seen nearby any of those places, then I will be sent to the Colonies.'

Hearing these words, I stared at him wonderingly. That, of course, was why 'Mr Sylvester' had seemed so much against the queen. It wasn't that he was secretly plotting against her, or had Catholic sympathies, but merely that she had caused him to be parted from the woman he loved and their child.

'That's why I'm working as a tutor in the magician's house – which happens to be not far from several of Her Grace's palaces – so that I can see Mistress Pryor, and our child, whenever possible.'

'Excuse me asking, but did I see you at the palace yesterday?' I suddenly interrupted.

He nodded and smiled wryly. 'I felt it safe, amongst so many, to go there in disguise. And Mistress Pryor and I had a carriage from there to bring us here to Putney.'

'*You* were in that carriage too?' I asked. 'I was

hanging on the back!'

He nodded. 'Yes, I was there, but we walked separately to this convent.'

'So perhaps it was you, then, who followed me along the dark passageway?'

'Possibly, though I had no idea I was following *you*.'

'And what of your tale, Mistress?' Tomas asked. 'For although I have no cause to question you, I'm very intrigued as to how you've managed yourself in all this.'

Mistress Pryor shrugged. 'It's been most difficult. I begged Her Grace to change her mind and let me marry the man I loved, but she said I could only marry when she allowed it, and then it would be to a man of her choosing.'

I gasped. 'That's very hard.'

'It is! But I'm still loyal to my lady and love her dearly. I would never betray her!'

'Of course not,' Tomas soothed.

'Leo and I continued to see each other, and eventually I found myself with child.'

'And you managed to conceal your condition?' I could not resist asking.

She sighed. ''Twas not easy, but many a lady has concealed such a matter under her farthingale. And . . . and in September, when my time was near, Her Grace and the Court went on a progress and I came here to give birth.' As she said this she looked at Mr Sylvester, such a look as to make anyone's heart break, for the love between them was palpable.

'And since then?' Tomas asked gently.

'Since then I have led a tragic life,' she burst out, 'for I am separated from my true love and also my babe, and there is no worse suffering for a mother.'

'But I'm sure they are kind to her here,' I said.

She began weeping again. 'They are kind enough, but this is a home for foundlings and there are above twenty homeless children, some orphaned, sick, crippled or simple. The few nuns who work here cannot give them a mother's love!'

We were all silent for a while, then Tomas said, 'In time, if Her Grace marries, then her feelings may mellow.'

'I cannot wait that long!' Mistress Pryor said. 'Every day away from my child is like a dagger in my heart. I only live for the time spent in this place.'

'But your coming here is most dangerous,' Tomas said. 'If the queen should discover that you have gone against her wishes, and have a child out of wedlock, then she may have you sent to the Tower.'

Mistress Pryor clutched at Mr Sylvester's hand. 'I know, and fear that very punishment above all others, for then my darling babe would be taken away from me!' Saying this, she burst out weeping again, and even Tomas and I vowing on our lives that no one should learn her secret from us did not stem her tears.

I took Tomas's hand, and such was the strength of my feeling in this matter that it did not seem overly bold. 'Do you not have the ear of the queen?' I asked him fervently. 'Would it not be possible for you to speak to her on this subject and obtain permission for Mistress Pryor to marry?'

Tomas sighed. 'In these matters, the queen is stubborn and always has been. Someone tried to address her on behalf of Mistress George – she who is even now in the Tower – but Her Grace merely stamped her foot and said that as she was single, her ladies must remain so.'

'But the queen is most fond of you,' I pleaded. 'Is there nothing you can say to help?'

Tomas thought for several moments, slowly shaking his head. 'At the moment, with her own love life so much spoken of, I dare not address her on the subject of marriage. In the meantime, however, perhaps I can devise a method whereby you are able to see more of little Elizabeth.'

Mistress Pryor looked up from her kerchief. 'Really? How could that be?'

'With some Tom-fool trickery,' Tomas said, smiling, and on hearing this, Mistress Pryor could not restrain herself, and leaving the side of Mr Sylvester, ran to Tomas and flung her arms around his neck.

Chapter Seventeen

Tomas had promised to try and fulfil this vow to Mistress Pryor by Twelfth Night and, though he hadn't confided in me the means he was going to use, he had also promised that I might play a part in it. Consequently, Twelfth Night saw me waiting anxiously behind a large folding screen in the palace banqueting hall, where I was due to appear before the Court as a representation of Winter in a court masque. I was dressed in floating panels of fine white muslin, standing behind girls similarly attired in gauzy yellow for spring, pink for summer and bronze for autumn. My role was a very small one, for the Seasons did not have to sing or dance, and, despite my fears about my appearance, I was happy to have another chance of being near to Her Grace, and of determining how Tomas was going to work his own particular magick.

My spying mission was over. I had not saved the

queen's life nor discovered any plot against her, and the day's task was not a mighty one concerning queen and country, but one involving just two people and a child. I felt it was, nevertheless, exceedingly important.

'Are you ready?' Tomas whispered to me. He had a beard longer and whiter than that of Dr Dee, his cloak was full, black and patched with many colours, and he wore a laurel wreath on his long grey wig. He was Olde Father Time, the central figure of the pageant.

I nodded, too overawed to speak.

'Now. Do you *really* know it's me?' he asked in my ear.

I nodded assuredly, for I'd seen him don his wig, beard and cloak in the small withdrawing room and there had been no opportunity since for him to have been replaced by someone else. He smiled at me, his stage-paint creasing and cracking, and I managed to smile back, wondering when I'd see him as his real self again, with no disguising nor masquerading. He looked magnificent, but I would a hundred times rather have had beside me the lad I'd ridden with to Putney.

On the other side of the screen to us, in the hall, was Her Majesty the Queen, together with the most important members of her Court, those maids of honour and ladies-in-waiting who weren't appearing in the masque and a selection of foreign dignitaries. They sat on gilt chairs facing a low stage which had been overlaid with grass of unnatural greenness and contained twelve painted wooden clouds, each representing a month of the year and having a girl dressed in filmy sky blue standing beside it. As each of these clouds had 'floated' on to the stage, the girl accompanying it had spoken a pretty rhyme in praise of her month.

The Sun, Moon and Stars were also there and these were represented by gentlemen ushers robed in silver and gold. Climbing on to the stage, they'd each spoken in turn and likened themselves to the queen, shining down on the people as she did and warming them with the light of her love. Each act was greeted with great acclaim by those in the hall.

'Now!' Tomas said at last to Spring, and with her leading the way (the Seasons, thankfully, having no words to speak apart from declaring their names) we joined those onstage.

Breathless, I looked up and above the heads of those seated in front of me, fixing my eyes on a point at the back, close to the painted ceiling, and only knowing where the queen was sitting by the fierce diamond-blaze of her jewels sparkling in the light of the room's innumerable candles. It had been rumoured that Her Grace's French suitor was sitting somewhere in the audience, and I longed to look along the rows for a small, pock-marked man – but that would not have been seemly.

The musicians struck up a seasonal tune and the ladies onstage who represented the months of the year did a dainty dance, forming themselves into fours, twos and sixes with practised ease. They came to rest, curtseyed before the dignitaries and received applause. When this died away the musicians struck up anew and the audience let out a collective 'Aaah!' of recognition as Olde Father Time appeared: a stooped figure with an hour-glass hanging on a leather strap around his waist.

And a swaddled infant steeping in his arms.

He declared:

'The old year dies – but only look
The young one cometh fast,
And we must to the future look
And never to the past!'

'Welcome to the New Year!' he cried, and so saying, put down the babe on the sward of grass and bowed low before the queen. The tableau was complete.

Loud applause and cheering followed, then Olde Father Time trudged wearily away. The applause being renewed, he returned to the stage and, after bowing once more, escorted each cloud-girl in turn to the front, where she curtseyed low and was led off. I and the other Seasons were then escorted off by the gentlemen ushers, leaving – alone onstage – little Elizabeth, still asleep.

For a moment people didn't seem to notice her and things continued as normal: ladies went to get changed, the gentlemen ushers began to disrobe and those outside in the banqueting hall could be heard voicing their approval of the masque and wondering what entertainment was coming next. Tomas and I exchanged glances; mine was anxious, for I still did not know what was in his mind.

After a moment we heard someone outside call, 'There is the babe still left here!' and Tomas winked at me.

A little later came another such cry, and then the queen herself, her tone very amiable, called, 'Where is my fool? Or should I say, where is Olde Father Time?'

Tomas went on to the stage once more and, throwing his beard over his shoulder with a flourish, bowed before the queen.

'Tomas,' said Her Grace, 'we enjoyed your pretty play, but it seems you have forgotten to remove one of the characters.'

Tomas looked towards little Elizabeth and pretended surprise. 'Ah yes. The New Year.'

'Whose child is she?' said the queen, adding, 'We presume it is a *she*?'

'She is, Your Grace, and named Elizabeth,' said Tomas.

The queen nodded graciously in acknowledgement of this.

'As to whose child she might be . . .' He shrugged. 'She is no one's child, for she comes from a home for foundlings.'

'And is she not to return there?'

'Perhaps,' Tomas said, affecting carelessness. He looked towards me. 'Is there someone here from the home to take her back?'

I came around the screen and bobbed a curtsey. 'There is not,' I said. 'I believe they have gone without her.'

'Ah. I suppose one babe more or less is nothing to them,' said Tomas.

'But that seems most cruel!' interjected the queen.

'Maybe so,' he said. 'But then a child must learn early that life is hard, and for those with neither family nor patronage 'tis even harder.'

'So this child has no one to care for it?'

'I believe no mother, father, aunt nor uncle,' said Tomas, to some gasps from ladies-in-waiting. 'No one in the world.'

I saw some of the foreign gentlemen shaking their heads. One said, 'This is very sad, and would not happen in my country.'

'Is there nothing we can do for her?' one lady-in-waiting asked, and I didn't have to look to the voice to know who it was.

'Yes! We will care for her at Court!' said the queen of a sudden. 'We will nurture this brave symbol of the New Year and hope that she'll return our love by bringing us good luck and a generous harvest.'

Courtiers, gentlemen and ladies-in-waiting alike applauded this notion, some of them calling, 'Bravo!'

'Well said, Your Grace,' said Tomas, smiling through his false beard. 'Shall I give the infant to your ladies to care for?'

'Indeed,' said the queen, basking in the approbation

of those around her. 'There are many ladies and only one babe, so 'twill not be an onerous task.'

Tomas signalled to me and I picked up little Elizabeth and carried her over to a group of ladies. I did not, however, give her to Mistress Pryor, for I felt that would have been too direct a statement. I looked at her, however, then had to look away quickly before I began weeping at the sheer joy on her face.

Chapter Eighteen

'Are you ready?' Tomas offered me his hand and, taking it, I stepped down the three stone steps into the small chapel. I'd left my cloak in the porch to make Miss Charity's blue gown look the better (she would, I knew, be delighted when I told her that it was being worn for a wedding) and my hair was loose and dressed with ribbands.

The chapel was a private one attached to a manor house at Barnes, quite close to where Sir Francis Walsingham lived. Being a privately-owned place of worship, it had escaped alteration when the queen's father had changed the religion from Catholic to Protestant, so still had the earlier faith's stained-glass windows, elaborate carved altar rails and shiny brass candlesticks. It was not yet six of the clock on a dank January morning and very dark outside, so two torches flamed on its walls and the altar was bright with candles.

As we walked a little further down the aisle and the light from these candles fell upon me, Tomas took in my appearance and smiled. 'So early in the morning to be dressed so grand!'

At the appreciative look in his eyes I lowered my head, feeling myself blush, for I was still unaccustomed to being with the real, true Tomas. He, too, looked very fine that morning, for he was wearing silken hose, a doublet of dark blue with silver threads woven through, and under, a gauzy lawn shirt gathered into smocking with a ruff at the neck.

'Did you have trouble getting away from the house?' he asked.

I shook my head. 'My girls are still asleep – and I'll be back before the household stirs.'

'And not one of them will have any knowledge of the ceremony which is about to occur! But what of Mistress Midge?'

'I told her I had an important errand to run for Mr Sylvester.'

Tomas, still holding my hand, squeezed it. 'And so you have.'

There was a movement to the right of us and a dark-robed parson appeared from the shadows to wish me good morrow. I continued to hold Tomas's hand tightly, partly because I was apprehensive about the occasion, and partly because I very much liked doing so.

Tomas introduced me. I made my curtsey and the

parson nodded in acknowledgement. 'And your two friends?' he asked. 'Are they come yet?'

Tomas answered that they would be here very shortly, and the parson moved back into the shadows where stood a table and chair. We heard the noise of a parchment being unrolled, then the scratching of a quill. 'I had to bribe him,' Tomas whispered to me. 'He wasn't keen on a marriage without the banns being called, but I persuaded him otherwise.'

'And do you think . . .' But before I had a chance to finish my question there was a noise at the door and Mr Sylvester and Mistress Pryor appeared. As they stepped into the light from the torches we saw that he was cheery, smiling, while she, wearing a silk gown in Tudor green, looked rather shy and demure. These attitudes were appropriate in each of them, of course, for it was their wedding day.

The marriage ceremony was soon over: the parson gabbled his words, making it as brief as possible in order to be finished before the household whose chapel it was came for morning prayers. Tomas and I stood as witnesses and signed the register, and (I'd been practising) I was proud to pen *Lucy Walden* with an adept hand and a flourish to each capital letter.

The parson, urging us not to tarry over-long, left the chapel. We congratulated the happy couple and the new Mistress Sylvester bent to kiss my cheek to thank me, then, turning to Tomas, voiced the question which

I'd tried to ask before the ceremony.

'Tomas. Do you really think Her Grace will forgive us?'

'Yes, what do you say to our chances?' said Mr Sylvester.

Tomas looked at them consideringly. 'Having been in the royal household all my life, I believe I know a little of Her Grace's feelings and attitudes,' he said. 'Certainly since having the little Frenchman for a lover, she's become more relaxed in her outlook – there are even rumours that she is about to release Mistress George from the Tower.'

'But how long do you think it will be before we can live together as husband and wife?'

'And mother and father of little Elizabeth?' added Mistress Pryor with some anxiety.

'We must take things slowly,' Tomas said, 'and be prepared for a setback if the rumours about Robert Dudley turn out to be true.'

'Indeed,' said Mr Sylvester.

'The first and most important thing has been to secure your child's legitimacy by legalising your union,' Tomas went on.

Mr Sylvester nodded and smiled, looking to his wife. 'And we have done this today.'

'You have,' said Tomas. 'And I believe the next thing will be for you, Mistress Sylvester, to withdraw from Court life as much as possible, perhaps setting up your own household. After a reasonable period, having made sure that Her Grace is in a compliant and agreeable mood – and certainly if she accepts the proposal of the French duke – I shall ask her if she might consider releasing you from her service.'

'And if she does not?' Mistress Pryor asked, then added quickly, 'But I shall not think on that, for today is my wedding day and I am determined to stay hopeful and happy!'

'That's the way, my sweetness!' Mr Sylvester said, putting an arm about her shoulders. He smiled at us. 'I fear there will be no wedding breakfast, but I've prepared a flagon of bride-ale and I suggest we take a walk to the lych-gate and drink a toast or two there before we return to our respective lives.'

And this we did, and were all a little merry by the hour of sun-up. At this time, however, I became anxious about getting home before the Dee family rose and discovered I was missing, so Tomas walked with me back to Mortlake. It was not far, but we strode briskly and I was out of breath by the time we reached the magician's house. By then, I was also feeling a little tearful, because the Court – and Tomas, of course – was due to move to Whitehall the following day and I felt my life would prove very dull and empty for the next few months.

We paused on the riverbank, where the river was high and a watery sun was just showing through cloud.

'So this is farewell,' he said.

I nodded. 'I know I may not see you for some time.'

He shrugged. 'Some considerable time. Who can tell? After Whitehall Her Grace usually goes to Windsor or Eltham, and then on summer progress to see some of her country-dwelling subjects.'

'And her fool always goes too.'

'Of course.'

'Then . . .' I felt a prickling at the back of my eyes and tried hard not to give way to tears, for I had no reason at all to presume that there was anything more than friendship between us. There had been no promises, no words spoken, no kiss. 'Then I may not see you for some months, Tomas. Nigh on a year, perhaps . . .'

'Ah,' he said, with some weight to this word.

I looked at him, frowning slightly. 'What do you mean?'

'Just that. *Ah.*'

'And what does *"Ah"* mean?'

He smiled broadly. 'It means that we'll see each other long before a year, Lucy, for I happen to know that in this month of January Dr Dee and his household are taking temporary lodgings in Whitehall in order to be near to the queen.'

I gasped. 'Never!'

He nodded. 'And there is already a certain matter awaiting your attention.'

'There is?' I asked.

He smiled. 'You may remember that we've never found the false Jack Frost: the varlet – or indeed the wicked young doxy – who impersonated me.'

'Of course! Do you think, then, that he'll be at Whitehall?'

'For sure he'll be wherever the Court is, spying and eavesdropping and trying to gain access to its secrets.'

'And I shall be there too. In London!' I stopped, fearful excited – and then had a thought. 'This is not another of your jests, is it?'

'It is not.'

'Truly?'

'By my troth, no.' He took my hand. 'And, Lucy, you look so lovely in your delight that I'm sorely tempted to kiss you.'

My heart gave a great leap. *At last!* I thought, and closed my eyes and tilted my face up towards his in readiness. Twelfth Night had come and gone and the kissing bough had been consigned to the fire, but it was never too late for kisses.

'I say I am *tempted*,' Tomas continued, 'but of course I would not venture to kiss a maid in such a public place for fear of ruining her reputation . . .'

'Oh!' Quite horrified, my eyes sprang open again – in time to see Tomas's lips coming towards my own.

'My sweet, I am jesting,' he murmured. And then we spoke no more until Mistress Midge rapped sharply on the kitchen window and I hurried in.

Whitehall. London. Close to Her Grace and close to Tomas. I could not ask for more . . .

Some Historical Notes from the Author

The Queen and Her Suitors

This book is set sometime during the start of the second half of Elizabeth I's reign, when she was in her early forties. At this time her ministers had not given up hope that she would marry and even, perhaps, provide the heir that England so needed. Various suitors appeared from all over Europe and the queen, while accepting their gifts and their professed love, played one off against the other, trying to gain the best deal for England and also foreign support in the event of a war. It seems she was especially fond of the French Duke of Anjou, for their courtship was an on-and-off affair which went on for months. They exchanged presents and rings, and once the queen actually announced to her ministers that they were betrothed. He was seventeen years younger, though, and her ministers were not happy that she was marrying a Frenchman and a Catholic, so eventually it came to nothing.

There was much public speculation about who might or might not be her lover, and Robert Dudley, Earl of Leicester and Master of the Queen's Horse, was a long-term favourite. His first wife died in suspicious circumstances, causing him to be hurriedly sent from Court and, eventually giving up hope that the queen would marry him, he secretly wed the Countess of Essex, one of her ladies-in-waiting.

The Real Dr Dee

Dr Dee was a mathematician, linguist and scholar – but was also very gullible. Kelly, his 'scryer', purported to speak to angels who gave him details of how to turn base metal into gold (by using the so-called 'philosopher's stone'), but unfortunately these details were in a strange angelic language which could never be properly deciphered. Dr Dee collected books from all over the world and was said to have the largest library in the country. As court astrologer he was frequently con-

sulted by the queen –
once, after a wax image of
her was found lying in
Lincoln's Inn Fields with a
great pin through its eyes. He
was able to assure her that it
had no powers to harm her and
generally calmed her superstitious fears.

Court Entertainments

These were lavish and costly and usually included
music and singing, dance and fireworks. When the
queen went 'on progress' around her kingdom, staying
at her richest subject's castles and stately homes, the
owners would spend an astonishing amount of money
on rebuilding, refurbishing and generally providing
extravagant diversions and attractions, inside and out,
in order to entertain her and her Court. These ranged
from plays, music, fireworks, bear-baiting and jousting,
to the half-moon-shaped lake which the Earl of
Hertford dug in his grounds for a lavish water pageant,
during which the 'lady of the lake' recited poetry
specially composed for the occasion, and little boats
sailed between miniature islands. Sometimes as many
as a thousand people would accompany the queen on
her progresses, and of course catering and accommo-
dating this great number could sometimes bankrupt
even an extremely wealthy man.

Puritans

Puritans were an extreme type of Protestant who sought purity in life and in worship. They dressed plainly, usually in black and white, and disliked any ornamentation or decoration on their persons or in their churches. In this they were at the opposite end of the scale to Roman Catholics, whose churches were rich with stained-glass windows and had candles in shiny candlesticks, decorative carvings and lace altar cloths.

Mary Queen of Scots

Mary was cousin to the queen and had a good claim to the throne. She and her supporters were thorns in Elizabeth's side for most of her reign. Various plots to unseat the Protestant Elizabeth and replace her with the Catholic Mary were hatched and discovered (sometimes by one of Sir Francis Walsingham's team of spies) until in 1886 Elizabeth had had enough and signed her cousin's death warrant.

Frost Fairs

The earliest recorded frost fair on the Thames was in 1309 when there were sports, dancing, a bonfire and a hare hunt on the ice. Later, frost fairs grew in content and sophistication and became much like the street fairs held in summer months. In the seventeenth century a printing press was erected on the frozen Thames, near London Bridge, and for a small fee you could take home a souvenir card printed with your name to prove you'd been there. (In the Museum of London there's one such card recording the fact that King Charles II and his family attended a frost fair on 31 January 1684.)

The Ladies-in-Waiting

These ladies, and the more intimate maids of honour, formed an elegant and decorative backdrop to the person of the queen, providing support, entertainment, advice and good company for Her Grace. Girls from titled families sometimes entered the Court aged about twelve and, after serving the queen for a number of years, were found suitable husbands. The queen did not approve of marriage for all, however, and was known to punish her ladies by sending them to the Tower if they fell in love with someone she didn't approve of – or someone whose attentions she wanted for herself. After she discovered that one of her ladies, the Countess of Essex, had been secretly married to

Robert Dudley and was also pregnant, she banished them both and, although he later came back into favour, she never received the new Lady Leicester, whom she thereafter referred to as the 'she-wolf'.

Mistress Midge's Favourite Recipes

Clotted Cream

Take a gallon of new milk from the cow, two quarts of cream, and twelve spoonfuls of rose water, put these together in a large milk pan, and set it upon a fire of charcoal well kindled (be sure the fire be not too hot) and let it stand a day and a night; then take it off and remove cream with a slice or scummer (let no milk be in it). Lay it in a cream-dish, with sugar scraped thereon, and so serve it up.

Flowers of All Sorts, Pickled

Put them into a preserving jar with as much sugar as they weigh, fill this up with wine vinegar. To a pint of vinegar put a pound of sugar and a pound of flowers. Keep them to decorate salads and boiled meats.

Apple Puffs

Take a large pippin (cooking apple) and mince it small with a dozen or so raisins. raisins. Beat in two eggs, season with nutmeg, rose water, sugar and ginger. Drop them into a frying pan with a spoon, fry them like eggs, squeeze on the juice of an orange or lemon and serve them up.

Apple Cream

Take a dozen pippins, pare, slice or quarter them, put them into a skillet with some some claret wine, a piece of ginger sliced thin, a little lemon peel cut small and some sugar. Let all these stew together till they be soft, then take them off the fire and put them into a dish, and when they be cold, take a quarter of boiled cream with a little nutmeg and put in of the apple as much as will thicken it, and so serve it up.

Glossary

booby – a foolish person

brazier – a small container for hot coals, used for cooking/heating

ceruse – a white lead pigment used as make-up

coffer – a box or chest for keeping valuables

coster – someone who sells fruit or vegetables from a barrow or stall

equerry – an officer in the royal household

ewer – a pitcher with a wide spout and handle for pouring

farthingale – a hoop or framework worn under skirts to shape and spread them

gallendine – a dark-coloured sauce made with vinegar, breadcrumbs, cinnamon, etc.

gee-gaw – decorative trinket; a bauble

Groat – English silver coin worth four old pence, used from the 14th century to the 17th century

kirtle – the skirt part of a woman's outfit. During this time everything (skirt, bodice, sleeves, ruff) came separately and were pinned together during dressing

link-boy – a boy who carried a torch for pedestrians in dark streets

litter – a man-powered form of transport, consisting of a chair or couch enclosed by curtains and carried on a frame or poles

malmsey – a sweet wine

marchpane – the old word for marzipan

mayweed – a flowering plant with a daisy-like head, also called dog fennel

neocromancer – sorcerer, black magician. One who tries to conjure up the dead

posset – a drink of hot milk curdled with ale or beer, flavoured with spices; a common recipe for treating colds

Rhenish – a dry white wine

ribband – a ribbon

samite – a heavy silken fabric, often woven with gold or silver threads

sarcenet – fine soft silk fabric used for clothing and ribbons

scry – to see or divine, especially by crystal-gazing

simples – medicines made from herbs

spinet – a type of small harpischord

taffety tart – a dish made with cream (the cream said to resemble the sheen of silk taffeta)

trencher – wooden or pewter plate for serving or cutting food

Bibliography

Brown, Maisie, *Barnes and Mortlake Past*
Historical Publications Limited, 1997

Fell Smith, Charlotte, *John Dee 1527–1608*
Constable and Company, 1909

Jenkins, Elizabeth, *Elizabeth the Great*
Phoenix Press, 1958

Picard, Liza, *Elizabeth's London*
Phoenix, 2003

Reed, Nicholas, *Frost Fairs on the Frozen Thames*
Lilburne Press, 2002

Weir, Alison, *Elizabeth the Queen*
Pimlico, 1999

Williams, Neville, *The Life and Times of Elizabeth*
Book Club Associates, 1972

Woolley, Hannah, *The Gentlewoman's Companion* (1675)
Prospect Books, 2001